"What ELIA KAZAN has done m___ times before in moving pictures, he has now accomplished with moving words."
—Budd Schulberg

AMERICA AMERICA

These words are the vision of a young man, Stavros Topouzoglou, twenty years old and ablaze with the dream of a new, far-off world.

Reaching for fulfillment and reality, he takes a journey that carries him across an ocean of experience, across a lifetime of passion and violence.

"An astonishingly moving narrative . . . beautiful."
—Orville Prescott
New York *Times*

AMERICA AMERICA was originally published at $4.95 by Stein and Day.

AMERICA

By ELIA KAZAN

AMERICA

with an introduction by
S. N. BEHRMAN

POPULAR LIBRARY • NEW YORK
Ned L. Pines • President
Frank P. Lualdi • Publisher

POPULAR LIBRARY EDITION
Published in February, 1964

Published by arrangement with Stein and Day, Publishers
Stein and Day edition published in November, 1962
Three printings

This book has also appeared in Italian, French, British,
Danish, Greek and Japanese editions.

*The characters and events in this book are fictitious, and any re-
semblance to real persons, living or dead, or actual events is entirely
coincidental.*

To my uncle
Avraam Elia Kazanjoglou
known as Joe Kazan

THE EFFRONTERY OF A DIRECTOR
An Introduction

Among the more exquisite agonies must be listed
the apprehension that assails one when a close
friend, who has never written anything before,
sends you a work for your critical opinion. When
that friend happens to have achieved a lustrous
reputation in a closely related field, the agony
takes on an additional refinement. I could not
help but remember, when Mr. Kazan asked me
to read *America America,* a story told me by
Somerset Maugham about *his* friend, Winston
Churchill. Maugham had suddenly, about 1910,
blossomed out as a playwright. He had four plays
running simultaneously in London. On a week-
end party Churchill told him he had a wonderful

idea for a play. Wary, Maugham advised Winston to write it and then suggested a manager—his own, Charles Frohman—to whom to send it. In fact he offered to send it himself; he offered everything except to read it. But Churchill wished to *discuss* it with Maugham; it was a personal experience and, as he himself would probably be too busy to write it, he wished to make a collaborative arrangement with Maugham. There was nothing for it: they made a dinner date at the Athenaeum. Maugham approached that evening somewhat in the spirit with which I approached *America America*. Churchill's idea turned out to be arresting rather than malleable: he had booked a compartment on the night train to Edinburgh and gone to the lavatory. When he tried to get out the door was stuck; he simply couldn't open it. He pounded on the door to no avail. The noise of the train drowned it out. The train lurched and he was seized with panic that there might be a wreck. He had no personal fear but was worried that an idea he had about the resolution of some political crisis might be lost. He therefore scribbled it out on a memorandum pad he carried in his pocket and released it to the railroad ties so that it would not be lost to the world. That was it! Anyone who has received "wonderful ideas" for plays from amateurs will concede that this one is more promising than most. It was not promising enough for Maugham.

There are more beguiling literary diversions than reading someone else's work in manuscript. When *America America* arrived I was in the middle of *The Guns of August.* I felt resentment. What made this special situation more poignant was that I was at that moment trying—I suppose together with every other living playwright—to get Mr. Kazan to direct a play of my own. Equivocation, in a case like this, was out of the question. Why, I thought, as I sat with the unwanted child on my lap, does the most sought-after director in the world also have to *write!* As I pondered this effrontery, I grumbled to myself: *"I don't want to direct! I am content to write. Why must Kazan write?"* But I was hooked, as Maugham was at the Athenaeum, and I read it.

But if there is no agony more exquisite than apprehension, there is no delight more pleasurable than the surprise of discovery—the prospector's joy in hitting a pay-streak of pure gold. Some time afterwards I was told that Tennessee Williams had gone through an experience with *America America* somewhat analogous to my own. "I put off readin' it," he said, "till I ran out of readin' matter, and then I had to read it and you know it was GOOD!" My incredulity lasted for quite a while; for about sixty pages my reading was accompanied by an obbligato: "It's good, it's damn good, but he can't keep it up. He'll come a cropper any minute!" But about page sixty I gave myself up to *America America* completely. The theme was close to me personally; the script provided an extension and illumination of my own brooding over the years.

The theme is immigration. *America America* tells the story of a Greek youth, Stavros, festering under a cruel tyranny in his homeland and of his obsessive drive to come to this country. The combustive passion, the steel-character and the steel-will that have to be welded to make such an escape possible—an epitome of the unbelievable odds, from 1620 up to this minute, when the paper difficulties alone are more stringent than ever—these are mysteries which I had pondered privately ever since I can remember.

I was myself born in this country, but my parents and my older brothers were immigrants from Memel, where they had lived in the nightmare of Czarist persecution. I had, as a child in Worcester, Massachusetts, questioned my parents about their migration here but I could never find out much. I have brooded endlessly, trying to thread the dark corridors of what their lives must have been before they came here. When I saw, early in Mr. Kazan's manuscript, the Turkish soldiers setting fire to the Church in which the terrified Greeks and Armenians are huddled praying for salvation against the flames that were about to devour their sanctuary, I knew what my own parents must have felt. I have encountered since, in my European travels—in England and in Italy and in post-war Germany—the hunger of people to come to America, but this desire emanates from a hope of economic improvement. But for Stavros' people—as for my own—it was a matter of life and death. America represented a sanctuary to which no Overlord would set the torch. This exigency of choice has been a primary motive in the many waves of European emigration here. It constitutes a living tissue in the fabric of this country's life, in a vast web of mingled racial memory. I have never seen it dramatized. It is strange that no one has ever done it. Kazan has done it. It doesn't have to be done again.

When I first read *America America* it was called *The Anatolian Smile*. It referred to the smile with which Stavros confronts an inimical world; the smile of deference, the smile of conciliation, the smile to ward off a blow. "Captains, white folks, I ain't done nothin'," says Myles, the Negro, in Faulkner's story, to his captors, who do not even bother to tell him of what he is accused. It is not until a great climactic moment in Stavros' spiritual development, at the very end of the story, that Stavros spontaneously laughs; up till then he has smiled his "I-ain't-done-nothin'" smile, to ingratiate the enemy, as in Kafka, for an undefined crime. The crime of any minority under any tyranny is the crime of being *there* instead of somewhere else, or of being anywhere, of living. Stavros' perpetual smile is an apology for being alive.

Kazan has created (perhaps remembered) an extraordinary collection of vivid characters. Whether he remembered them or invented them, they are creations. Unlike Candide, who is stupid, Stavros is bright; he emerges from innocence; he learns the facts of life, among them that you have to kill a man before he kills you. On the road to Constantinople, moving through a miry nexus of corruption, Stavros encounters a wonderfully characterized bandit, who says to him:

> All you can do is smile and swallow. Just a bag of guts. I've killed men like you and it's no different than killing a sheep. One clean cut almost anywhere and the life flows out. A twitch or two and it's over. Have a drink! No! Of course! You don't drink. You don't fight. You've no use for women. What kind of a man are you?

Stavros shows him. He kills him. It is one of the most satisfying homicides in literature.

When the young murderer finally arrives in Constantinople, penniless, his education in the swelter of life only begins. He becomes part of the city's sewage. But even that sewage is iridescent, not only with decay, but with humanity. Garabet, for instance—a superb characterization —likes Stavros and wants to subtract sex from his other starvations. But the charity robs Stavros again of his pitiful savings toward passage to America. Out of his total disillusionment Garabet tries to educate Stavros: "Tell me!" he asks, "since you left home, have you met among your Christians, one follower of Christ? Have you met among human beings, one human being?"

"You," says Stavros.
"Me! Didn't you look in my face? You don't know me. You don't know what I am. . . . I have one idea for this world. Destroy it and start over again. There's too much dirt for a broom. It calls for a fire. It needs the flood."

From the cloaca Stavros emerges into the world of expediency. And here Kazan has managed to create, most engagingly, the atmosphere of a sweet bourgeois family and the lovely image of a sad and unsung and homely heroine, Thomna. Since he can't earn the money to go to America by hard work, Stavros has decided to marry it. Thomna is a darling but with, regrettably, a long nose. Stavros' Aunt, back home, looking at Thomna's photograph which Stavros has sent, says: "They say that a long nose is a sign of virtue," and his Uncle replies: "With a nose like that, virtue is inevitable." In the Dolce Vita of Constantinople, Stavros encounters an American rug millionaire and his wife, Sophia, and these two add to his education and contribute to his escape. The characters are all simmering with life; even the lost one, Hohanness, whose death is the gateway for Stavros' life.

A word about the style, which struck me: in its simplicity and emotional intensity it is Biblical. Stavros' family is deeply religious in the Christian tradition; they speak sparingly but everything they say glows with feeling. There is scarcely a word in this text that is not irradiated with emotion, primitive in the beginning and more complex after the young hero begins his wandering but, throughout, the actual words that the characters say seem to be distilled like a sharp liquor from subterranean streams of harsh experience and hidden pools of desire. It is true of the Tartuffian bandit Abdul, of the Voltairian porter Garabet, who speaks with the disillusionment of Ecclesiastes, of the sad and bartered bride Thomna, of the worldly secret drinker Sophia. The *Heimweh* for two countries —for the stark hills and family warmth of the Anatolian peninsula and for the other country, the unseen and golden shore of the not yet discovered and unattainable America—throbs like David's cry for Absalom. The boy Stavros is rent by two homesicknesses; for the home he has abandoned, for the home he seeks. It is the pain at the heart of every migration. But there is a high exaltation, too. Stavros makes it.

So does Kazan!

S. N. Behrman

*And they heard the soldiers shouting
"Thalatta! Thalatta!"*

—XENOPHON

1

THE BEGINNING

Turkey in Asia,
the land known as Anatolia

Mount Aergius is seen from a great distance, beautifully shaped, perfectly proportioned, its peak and sides covered with snow. We hear a song, the voices of two men. We do not get the words, for they are in another tongue.

High on the cool side of the mountain is an ice field. A wagon and an old horse are standing at its edge. Two men are cutting ice into manageable pieces.

The work is heavy, but they are young and strong. They labor in the rhythm of men who are working for themselves. Their voices, though untrained, blend pleasantly. Here is the rapport of close friends.

Stavros Topouzoglou is a boy of twenty. There

is something at once delicate and passionate about his face. It is full of inarticulated yearning. His brown eyes shine like moist olives.

Working next to him is Vartan Damadian. He is twenty-eight. His face has a wild, swarthy cast. An enormous nose, bent but defiant, a low forehead, hair of electric vitality, full sensuous lips. These features and his bearlike heft make him a formidable figure.

The two men are small figures against the ice-field. Behind them is a vast panorama. We hear the ominous sound of the wind that inhabits this plateau.

> *Once long ago, Anatolia was a part of the Byzantine Empire, inhabited by the Greek and Armenian people of that time. In 1381 this land was conquered by the Turks, and since that day the Greeks and the Armenians have lived here as minorities, subject to their Mohammedan conquerors.*

In the foreground a single telegraph wire is strung on a series of primitive poles which recede into the distance, emphasizing the effect of space.

Far back is Mount Aergius. Nearby a community of houses can be seen, built partly on the sides of two facing cliffs, partly in the narrow level between. This town is named Germeer. We notice a minaret or two.

This is the day of the holiday known as "Bay-ram," when every Turk who can afford it slaughters a lamb and offers part of the meat to the poor. A herd of sheep is being driven through a crowded street. The shepherd stops to sell one of his animals to a householder. Behind him his family is dressed in their holiday best. Drinks are being poured.

A tethered lamb bleats. He knows what's in store for him. As the drinks are passed among the other members of the family, the father is sharpening a kitchen knife. He is clearly very familiar with it both as a utensil and as a weapon.

The entire family is here. The women are in the doorway, their faces partly covered. They are all watching the head of the family dress a newly slaughtered animal. A little girl brings her father a drink on a small tray. He takes it, then kisses his child passionately.

Some well-dressed men gallop down the street on horseback. Women pull children to safety. Behind the riders, a brace of horses races, the driver crying a wild command. The horses veer away, the carriage following. At the front of the Municipal Building, men are arriving, some in carriages, some on horseback, some on foot, all dressed for the holiday. There is something threatening in the air.

Inside the Municipal Building, the Wali or governor of the province has summoned his council to an emergency meeting.

The door to the Wali's inner office is suddenly thrown open. Two soldiers, powerful men, come through, stamping their feet in a style taught them by the German military who trained the Turkish army. They set the stage for the entrance of a formidable man. Instead, through the door comes a worried little bureaucrat—the Wali.

The council members leap to their feet. The Wali hurries to his desk.

The Wali, querulously: "Be seated . . . please . . ."

The council members sit. The soldiers stand at fixed attention.

The Wali, complaining: "Where are my . . . ?"

An aide jumps as though his life depended upon it, and brings him his glasses.

The Wali unfolds a telegram: "This came on the wire from the Capital an hour ago." He reads, " 'Your excellency! On this day, the eve of our holy feast of Bayram, Armenian fanatics have dared to set fire to the National Turkish Bank in Constantinople.' "

The Wali looks up. Among the members of the council there is some sort of reaction, but not a clear one. Anger? Impatience? Some men simply sigh.

The Wali continues with the telegram: "'We have reason to believe it is the wish of our Sultan, Abdulhammid the Resplendent, the Shadow of God on earth, that the Armenian subject people throughout his empire be taught once and for all that acts of terrorism will not be tolerated. Our Sultan has the patience of the prophet, but he has now given signs that he would be pleased if this lesson were impressed once and for all upon this disorderly and dangerous minority. How this is to be effected will be left to their Excellencies, the Governors of each Province, and to the Army Commander in each Capital.'"

Behind the Wali, the soldiers are at attention, listening.

At the office of the Commander of the Army post, the Pasha, or General, a dark, bulky man, is finishing reading the same telegram to his staff.

An attendant brings him a water pipe. The Pasha puts the telegram down and sighs deeply. No army man likes to receive orders of this kind.

The Pasha, with sudden vehemence: "I will not send soldiers to do this!"

An officer: "There was writing again . . . insults . . . on the wall of the Mosque, your Excellency!"

A crowd has gathered in front of a small mosque. On the walls, some crude scrawls can be seen. A *hodja,* or holy man, comes out, with pail and brush to wash the markings off. The crowd mutters and curses. Elsewhere in the town, angry men are gathering. The entire Turkish community is furious.

Back on the cool, clean side of Mount Aergius, Stavros and Vartan have finished loading their wagon with ice, and now, weary, stand for a moment, looking up at Aergius. It is restful to look up at this fine mountain.

Stavros: "You say in America they have mountains bigger than that one?"

Vartan: "In America everything is bigger."

Stavros: "What else?"

Vartan: "What else what?"

Stavros: "What else in America? What else will we do when we get there?"

Vartan: "We'll stop talking about it for one thing. Let's go there, with the help of Jesus! Why do we let the days pass?" Then, seductively, "Come on you! Let's go you!"

Stavros looks at him with abject hero worship. He idolizes this man.

Vartan, brusquely: "Better sell this ice before it melts."

They finish covering their load with old scraps of rugs and cloths, leap on the wagon, and are off. The horse, since it is going downhill, manages a trot. Stavros notices something ahead. He points.

On the slope of the mountain below, a small encampment of soldiers sits at ease around campfires. An officer is walking out onto the road to intercept the wagon.

Vartan looks around for some escape. There is none.

Vartan: "A day's work for nothing!"

Stavros, under his breath: "Allah!" It is his favorite expression.

The officer, now in the middle of the road, holds up his hand, commanding the wagon to stop. The wagon stops. The officer walks around it.

Vartan, his head down: "Help yourself, sir. Help yourself."

There is just the least sarcasm in his tone. Vartan's game is to see how close he can come to saying what he thinks without endangering his life. He doesn't come very close, but this subtle game does save a little of his dignity.

The officer, at the back of the wagon, ignores or does not notice the effrontery. He turns and bellows toward the encampment.

Officer: "Chelal!!"

A soldier-cook runs out of the mess tent with some brass pots. Within seconds, a dozen soldiers are helping themselves to bits of ice from the wagon.

Vartan sits with his head still bowed, apparently uninterested in what's happening in the wagon behind him. Stavros looks at his hero anxiously. Then he decides to play Vartan's game, nudges him as if to say, "Watch!"

Stavros has turned in his seat in the direction of the officer.

Stavros: "Sir! Your honor!"

Vartan looks straight down his horse's back, waiting the incident out.

Stavros, a little bolder, speaks to the officer again: "Your honor!!"

The officer finally looks at him. Stavros quickly retreats behind a smile. This smile, the most characteristic thing about the boy, has a strong element of anxiety. It is so often the unhappy brand of the minority person—whether Negro, Jew, or yellow man—the only way he has found to face his oppressor, a mask to conceal the hostility he dares not show, and at the same time an escape for the shame he feels as he violates his true feelings.

Stavros: "Sir, help yourself, help yourself!"

Vartan, mumbling so that only Stavros can hear him: "That's what he needs. Encouragement!"

Stavros, flattering but insolent, to the officer: "But your honor . . ."

Officer: "What do you want?"

Stavros: "It is not I, your honor, it is the ice. Its nature is to melt. It does not consider that we have to go all the way to the market place to sell it."

Stavros smiles nervously. The officer is a vigorous and impulsive man. He is quick to anger, dangerous when aroused.

Officer: "In plain language, you want me to hurry?"

Stavros turns and looks at Vartan. But Vartan offers no help. All Stavros can do is smile!

The officer suddenly leaps on the wagon, begins to throw off big pieces of ice. In no time the wagon is half empty. Vartan barely takes notice. Stavros still holds his smile, but now we see how strained and anxious it is.

The officer leaps off the wagon. His men are convulsed with laughter. He responds to their laughter by moving toward the front of the wagon in a slow strut.

Officer: "You had too much of a load for this dear old horse. Now he'll get you to the market more quickly. Agree? Eh?"

Stavros looks at Vartan to see what he'll say. Vartan says nothing. Stavros is frightened. The officer demands an answer.

Stavros: "Yes, sir."

Officer: "What are you, Armenians?"

Stavros: "Greek, sir, a poor Greek."

Officer, to Vartan: "And you?"

Stavros looks at Vartan. Vartan does not raise his head.

Vartan: "I'm an Armenian."

Officer: "Oh, Armenian? Did you have anything to do with the burning of the State Bank yesterday in Constantinople?"

Vartan does not answer. Stavros is still holding the bag.

Officer, to Stavros: "Why do you smile?"

Stavros: "You're joking, your honor."

Officer: "Oh?"

Stavros: "Forgive me, but how could he have been in Constantinople yesterday? It's a two weeks' journey."

Officer: "Even with this horse?"

His men all laugh, appreciating his sadistic game. Stavros seems to join in. Suddenly Vartan leaps out of the wagon and walks toward the officer. Despite himself, the officer is startled and puts his hand to his sidearm.

Vartan, to the officer: "Captain Mehmet. You don't recognize me? We served together—eight years ago. That is, I served you, and you served the Sultan. I was your orderly, so naturally you have forgotten me. Remember, I stole chickens for you."

The officer looks Vartan straight in the face and for the first time sees him.

Officer: "Vartan? You?"

Vartan: "Yes, Vartan. The same."

The officer throws his arms around Vartan. A warm embrace. Stavros stares at Vartan with the purest hero worship!

Officer. "Vartan, my little lamb, what's happened to you?"

Vartan: "As you see—I'm trying to make a few coppers with this dear dying stud."

Officer, shouting: "Enver! Chelal! Put the ice back. Quickly! Come, jump! Before it melts."

The men begin to reload the wagon frantically. The officer draws Vartan to one side. Stavros steals up to hear their conversation.

Officer: "Your people burn our building and you expect us to thank you! No. Today no Armenian will be forgiven for being an Armenian. You better stay up here with me."

Stavros interrupts them: "He has his mother and his father down there. And his little brother."

The officer pauses: "Then it's in the hands of God."

In the town, people in terror are entering the Armenian Church. The front door is guarded from the inside and opened cautiously to admit the late arrivals. Hysterically frightened men and women crowd through the door as it is pulled shut. We get a glimpse of the panic within. After an instant the door is reopened just enough so that a boy of eleven can slip out of the sanctuary. He is Vartan's younger brother, Dikran. The door is immediately pulled to again and bolted.

On the road in the outskirts of town, Dikran, breathless from running, waves down Vartan's wagon. The boy leaps up on the driver's seat. There begins a frantic consultation in whispers.

Dikran: "But Vartan, father says come now!"

Vartan: "I have this ice to sell *now*."

Dikran: "You want me to say that to him?"

Vartan: "Yes. And get off the streets! Go back in the church. Dikran, go!"

When next seen the wagon is parked near a central square of the city. By now most of the ice has been sold. Stavros is dealing with an old Turkish woman. Vartan stands on the driver's seat, singing out.

Vartan: "Ice!! Little pieces of the mountain!! Mount Aergius ice!!"

The old woman pays Stavros, meantime speaking to him in a confidential tone.

Old Woman: "There's an old well under our house. He could hide there."

Stavros: "Vartan wouldn't do that."

Old Woman: "That's the way those Armenians are. You see! Well, he'll be dead soon."

She goes. Stavros looks up at Vartan. The ice is about gone. Vartan jumps down off the wagon seat.

Vartan: "You'd better go home now!"

Stavros: "And you?"

Vartan: "I'm going to the Guitars."

Stavros: "What for!"

Vartan: "I will drink with my murderers."

Stavros: "What for!!!????"

Vartan: "For my satisfaction!"

Stavros: "Allah!"

Then as he starts to protest again, Vartan points.

Vartan: "Your mother's coming!"

A woman about forty-five, her face covered in the traditional manner, is hurrying toward the wagon. She is Vasso Topouzoglou, Stavros' mother, and she is furious.

She goes up to Stavros, seizes him by the lobe of one ear and starts dragging him off. People take notice.

Vartan laughs. Vasso suddenly releases Stavros and turns to his companion.

Vasso: "Vartan, stay away from my son. Play games with your own life."

Then she goes back to Stavros and begins to drive him off before her.

Vasso: "What did your father tell you? Stay away from that man? Did he tell you that? Do you listen? Can you hear?"

Vasso, still in a fury, drives her son before her all the way to their house.

Inside it is almost dark. Around a single oil lamp huddle a dozen men, the leaders of the Greek community. Among them are Stavros' father, Isaac Topouzoglou, and a bearded Orthodox Priest. Vasso and Stavros enter.

Vasso: "Here he is, Isaac. Your eldest!"

Some men fall away and reveal Isaac. In his own home he sits like a king. He waits.

Vasso: "He was with the Armenian again."

Isaac doesn't answer. Stavros says nothing.

Vasso, to the boy: "You have given your father a day of terrible worry. Go kiss his hand and ask his forgiveness."

The boy starts toward his father.

Vasso: "He's too easy with you." Then to her husband: "You're too easy with him, Isaac. If you'll forgive me to say so, it's not my place to say so, but . . ."

The boy has reached his father and stands in front of him. The father suddenly whacks the boy across the face.

Vasso: "Good."

The father now extends this same hand to be kissed. Stavros kisses it.

Vasso: *"Good!"*

Then Isaac kisses the boy. Vasso nods her approval of this too. Thus the ceremony is completed.

Isaac, to Stavros: "Have you had dinner?"

Stavros: "I'm not hungry."

Vasso: "You will eat something."

She leaves for the kitchen.

The group huddles around the lamp.

A Man: "Who is this Armenian?"

Isaac: "Damadian's son, Vartan."

Men (a murmur of bees): "No good, he's no good, no good no good . . . no good at all . . ."

A Man: "He doesn't know his place!"

Stavros has been listening intently. What is being said infuriates him. Now he gets up and starts for the stairs.

Isaac: "Well—it's not our affair. They're Armenians. We're Greeks. Their necks are not our necks."

Stavros, on the stairs, as he goes up, has to speak.

Stavros: "True. They're saving our necks for

their next holiday."

He's up and out of sight.

Everyone is astonished at this remark, not only because of the sentiment expressed, but because of the sudden liberty Stavros has taken in the council of his elders.

One of the Men: "What! What did he say?"

The Orthodox Priest: "We all heard what he said."

A moment of bewilderment. Then all start talking at the same time, vehemently.

Isaac: "Shhhh!"

Instant silence. The men look toward the windows, anxiously, afraid they might be overheard by strangers. The discussion continues, now in a sort of whisper.

Stavros enters his bedroom, closes the door, goes to the window, opens it, and drops out into the night.

ぺぺぺ

The Guitars is a combination raki house, coffee house, and cabaret. The floor is of compacted dirt. The place is Turkish-owned, Turkish-operated. The patrons—at the moment overflowing the place—are *lumpen,* many drunk, all filthy.

They are vagabonds, hamals (porters), camel drivers, criminals, soldiers out of uniform, servants after hours. The lone woman present is a singer. And she is almost male. She is seated between a couple of guitarists, a match for them in any contest. She pushes a deep contralto voice through an "Aman" song. A couple of hamals are dancing on a small wooden floor in front of the musicians.

Stavros is looking for Vartan, and finds him in a corner, drinking alone at a table. Stavros sits.

Vartan drinks, then indicates the crowd: "The jails are empty!"

The music stops. The dancers leave the floor. Vartan gets up and starts toward the door. Stavros follows. Vartan goes to the musicians and, as is the custom, throws some coins at their feet. They begin to play. Stavros comes up and he and Vartan begin to dance, each solo but in the same rhythm, with the same feeling. There is great beauty in their slow, circular movements. And despite the fact that they are not looking at each other, we feel that they are dancing together.

Suddenly, at what seems to be a peak in their slow, somehow orgiastic turning, Stavros whispers.

Stavros: "America America!"

He says this as if it were one word and with the deepest yearning.

Vartan: "Are you ready?"

Stavros nods slowly.

Vartan: "Come on you!! Let's go you! If we don't go tomorrow . . ."

A couple of men have come up and have been talking to the musicians. All are looking at Vartan and Stavros. The music stops. Then the lead guitar player kicks the coins which Vartan has thrown at his feet off the platform. Everyone in the room stares at the two boys. A resounding silence. A pause. Then the sound of a commotion in the distance. Finally, a huge shout. A man runs in with news. There is much milling around.

Man, shouting: "It's beginning!"

Back at the Armenian Church, where the people have taken refuge, brush, old timber, and scraps of wood are being piled against the side of the building. Coarse shouts are heard. A fence is ripped up and added to the pile. A great shout. It is a sadists' holiday. Some soldiers—half out of uniform—are supervising.

Vartan and Stavros come up. Some boys, among them Dikran, gather around Vartan, awed, frightened. Dikran takes Vartan's hand. Vartan puts his arm around his little brother. Shouts, laughter, cheers are heard.

In front of the church, an army veteran, wearing the coat of his uniform, holds an old Armenian by the beard. His other hand brandishes a curved sword. The old man has his arms thrown out in a gesture of self-immolation.

Officer: "We don't want you, father. We want the ones who still carry the seed. Now go back in there and tell them to come out and beg for mercy."

He releases the old man, who glances at a window of the church. His wife is watching him. The old man picks himself up and chooses what will be the last act of his life.

He spits in the face of the officer.

This is the excuse that the Turkish officer has been waiting for. He shouts, "Aaahhtesh! AAH tesh!" (Fire! Fire!)

In the church window, the old woman watches her husband's quick death. Her eyes fill with horror as the officer's sword comes whacking down!

Soldiers immediately set fire to the piles of brush and timber around the church. The fires at the side of the church burn hungrily.

Inside, the church begins to fill with smoke. The Armenians, about fifty or sixty in number, are huddled around the altar praying. As the place begins to fill with smoke, they panic, children cry, men shout.

Outside, Stavros backs off a little, thoroughly frightened. Dikran and some other young boys are as close to the front door of the church as they can be, considering the fire and smoke.

Inside the church, as the building itself now begins to burn, there is pandemonium.

Vartan has a desperate plan for this emergency. Suddenly he screams "Dikran!" and throws himself on the Turkish officer, pulls a dagger out of the officer's belt, and stabs him. Then he wrestles free the man's pistol and starts holding off the men who come at him from all sides.

The front door of the church is left temporarily unguarded by Vartan's tactic. Dikran and some of the other little boys run and throw it open. People run out.

Murderous men cover Vartan. A pack of dogs on a fox. Stavros doesn't know what to do. Suddenly it is not possible to save Vartan. It is impossible.

People are rushing out of the front door of the Church in all directions—men, women, and children. The Turks take out after the Armenians, killing those they catch regardless of age or sex. A Turk shouts at the top of his lungs.

Turk: "The men! The men! Leave the women! The men! Get the men . . ."

It is a gray morning. Women in black have come to the burned out church for the bodies of their men. Vartan's body is covered with a piece of burned carpet. Stavros sits there, crying in chokes. In his hand, he holds Vartan's fez.

Stavros carries the body of his friend home. The Armenian section is ringed by Turkish soldiers "preserving order." The street is strewn with discarded household furnishings. Pillaging is still going on.

Stavros is exhausted. Vartan is very heavy. Stavros walks a few steps, stops, then a few more, leans against a tree, then on for a few more steps. Vartan's fez is still clutched in his hand.

Two Turkish guards see Stavros. One of them moves forward and trips the boy. The body falls and rolls heavily. Stavros gets up and starts to pick it up. But the two soldiers are on him. As they arrest Stavros, some women in black rush in, lift up the body of Vartan, and carry it off.

✿✿✿

At a large outdoor compound, which is part of the city prison, about fifty men, Armenians in all conditions of desperation, cover the ground. The place is filthy. Stavros sits holding Vartan's fez in his hands. A boot nudges him.

Voice: "Up!"

Stavros' father, Isaac, sits in the Wali's office in the attitude of a suppliant. In various corners of the office, members of the council discuss in whispers the events of the night before.

The conversation between the Wali and Isaac is private. The Wali passes Isaac some cologne to refresh his hands and face.

Wali: "Once these horrors start they must run their course. The patient man waits. As the Prophet said: hatred exhausts itself. It's no comfort for me that the Armenians started this. I believe that some day, with Allah's help, all races will live together in peace. Even the Armenians."

Isaac: "That's the hope of mankind."

Isaac can't help but look anxiously toward the door. The Wali notices this, laughs gently.

Wali: "They're bringing him, my friend. They're bringing him. Sit back in your chair! That's it. A smile? Eh?"

Isaac, smiling: "Yes, yes. I'm so grateful to you."

Wali: "So! It's not only that I like you. I like all the Greek subject people."

Isaac: "We all know that."

Wali: "I am here only for the good I can do. I make nothing here. You realize that."

Out of long habit, Isaac reaches into his pocket.

Wali: "And I do good. I *do* help. Don't you think?"

Isaac: "Oh, yes. We're all very grateful."

Wali: "I was referring particularly to you. You have a good business here. The Turkish people like you and you have a good business."

Isaac: "We make a living."

Wali: "I happen to know you do very well. And that makes me happy."

The door to the office is slowly opened. An attendant is standing there. He does not permit the door to open more than halfway. A soldier puts his head in and whispers to the attendant. Behind him Stavros can be seen. The attendant rushes halfway to the Wali, stops short. He speaks softly.

Attendant: "Your honor. Forgive me . . . but . . ."

Wali: "Hold him there a moment!!!"

Then he turns and looks at Isaac. Isaac's

hand now comes out of his pocket. Holding money! He stands. The Wali stands. An ancient ritual. Isaac bends over and kisses the Wali's hand. Simultaneously he presses money into the hand of the Turk.

Stavros, at the door of the office, takes in the incident. He's ashamed for his father. He watches as a servant with a tray of refreshments serves the members of the council. At a signal from the Wali, the servant offers a drink to Isaac. Isaac takes it. The members of the council, drinks in hand, move in towards their Governor. Isaac is surrounded. A toast is offered. They all drink except Isaac. Then one of the council members notices that Isaac is not drinking. He indicates with insistent conviviality that he must or else offend his hosts.

Stavros, in the doorway, watches to see what his father will do. Isaac, surrounded by the council members, drinks. What else could he possibly do? Laughter!

ʊʊʊ

Isaac and Stavros walk down the front steps of the Municipal Building. Stavros is looking at his father—with a new awareness. Suddenly

Isaac jerks his head up and looks at the boy. Stavros drops his eyes.

Isaac: "Stavros? What?"

The boy drops his eyes, keeps walking. Isaac falls behind, trying to puzzle out his son.

Stavros has come to a narrow side street. Abruptly, without explanation, he turns and disappears down this alley. Isaac runs to the head of the alley, calls.

Isaac: "Stavros! Stavros!"

Stavros now begins to run down the alley with demonic speed. In a second or two he is gone. Isaac turns and walks away. He is very troubled.

ننن

From very far away we see a great cliff. Long ago, the people who lived in this area built their homes into the sides of this cliff for safety from their enemies and from the roaming bandits who terrorized the plain. In time, many of these homes were abandoned and collapsed, but people still live in the ruins. At this moment the only thing that moves is a tiny figure, far below. It is Stavros, looking up and calling out.

Stavros: "Yaya! Yaya!" (Grandmother!)

In the rubble and among the scattered boulders of the ruins can be seen a decaying wooden structure. There is some sort of movement. A human figure appears in a doorway at the head of a cellar dwelling.

She is an old woman, seventy or more, but in full vigor. Her face is dehydrated meat. We hear Stavros yell "Yaya!" again. The old woman watches the approaching boy without a sign of welcome. The air above is full of pigeons.

As Stavros approaches, he waves. His grandmother makes no sign, merely stares at the boy. Stavros comes up, smiling.

Grandmother: "What do you want?"

Stavros: "I came to see you, Yaya."

Grandmother: "What for? You don't look well. How's that good Greek, your father? You know why the fox loves the rabbit? Because it's got no teeth. How's your father? Your grandfather was a man! I've been expecting you. He told me you were coming."

Stavros: "Who?"

Grandmother: "Your grandfather. He came to see me last night. I think he found a new wife in the land of the dead. Well, what can you do?! But he still comes to see me. What's the matter?"

Stavros: "Nothing. Why?"

Grandmother: "You're moving around like a criminal. What do you want?"

Stavros: "I just came to see you."

Grandmother: "You're lying. My God, I hope you're not going to be like your father. You already have his smile. Well! What can you do?! All the men in our family lie now. The Turk spits in their face and they say it's raining. Well? Say! What have you come for? And don't lie again because your grandfather told me what you wanted."

Stavros: "What did he tell you I wanted?"

Grandmother: "Money. True? Say!"

Stavros: "True."

Grandmother: "Why should I give you money?"

Stavros: "What do you need it for? You're an old woman!"

She picks up a stick and begins to hit him with all her might.

Grandmother: "Go on, go on, get out, get out!"

Stavros takes the stick from her and breaks it.

Stavros: "Now you're going to listen to me. I'm going away."

Grandmother: "Good!"

Stavros: "Far away."

Grandmother: "The farther the better."

Stavros: "To America. I'm going to America."

Grandmother: "You!"

Stavros: "You're not going to see me again!"

Grandmother: "You! You'll stay at your father's side. You're a good boy."

Stavros: "Only give me enough to get to Constantinople. There I'll work and make the rest. Hear me! You are my only hope. Don't turn your back on me!!"

Suddenly the old woman turns and goes into her cellar dwelling. Stavros follows.

The cellar is very small and packed with everything she has ever had and valued. When Stavros enters she is down on her knees, searching in the back of an old chest.

Grandmother: "I remember you as a baby, soft and round, made of butter. And I remember you in that little blue sailor suit your mother made you. A saint with a blessed pale face, your eyes shining with God's own light."

Stavros' face does indeed have innocence and purity.

She pulls out an object wrapped in some cloths.

Grandmother: "Oh, I thought, Oh if only the world were like that!!"

She has unwrapped the cloth and now holds up a murderous curved dagger. Her voice is hard now.

Grandmother: "Here! It was your grandfather's."

Stavros: "Oh God, I don't need this! I need money."

Grandmother: "You need this more. Take it. It will remind you no sheep ever saved his neck by bleating."

Stavros snatches the dagger from her: "All right! I'll walk into the city and I'll put this into the first soldier I meet and . . ."

Grandmother: "Stavros, you can't frighten me."

Suddenly the frantic boy begins to rip up the planks, the pieces of metal, the old rags and bits of rug which cover the floor. His grandmother watches sardonically for a moment.

Grandmother: "It's here . . . under my clothing."

She indicates her middle, stands there, stooped, bent, challenging. Stavros, dagger in hand, stares at her. For a moment it appears he might rip her open. He walks slowly towards where she stands. Then the moment passes.

Grandmother: "You're not going to America. You're your father's son. Go home. Be what you are."

She turns her back on him and slowly begins to stuff back into the chest the articles she took out. A cry breaks from the boy—frustration, grief, fury at himself. Then still holding the dagger, he leaves.

Stavros walks, taking the road back to the city. The sun is setting. Coming up behind him and about to overtake him is a young man, gaunt as a board: Hohanness Gardashian. He is pitched in perpetual motion forward. His clothes, all tatters and patches, are saturated in dust. A small pack is tied to his back. His face is alight with the most perfect hope.

Hohanness goes past Stavros. Then he stops, taken with a fit of coughing of such intensity that he crouches at the side of the road to "ride it out." It subsides as Stavros comes up to him, and Hohanness turns, extends one hand, smiles . . .

Hohanness: "Anything! Anything!"

Stavros, not in the mood to think of anyone else, shakes his head, almost viciously, and goes on.

Hohanness, from behind him: "Hear me . . . I'll remember you. From America, I'll pray for you."

Stavros stops short and turns. Hohanness is still crouched at the side of the road . . . smiling.

Hohanness, extending a hand: "Anything, anything . . ."

Stavros, going back to him: "You go to America . . . you!"

Hohanness: "With the help of Jesus."

Stavros: "On foot?!"

Hohanness: "However."

Stavros: "And with nothing?!"

Hohanness: "Each day. Part of the distance."

Stavros glares at him. He is bitterly jealous.

Stavros: "How are you going to get there with those?? Eh??"

He indicates Hohanness' shoes, which are flapping out their last days. Hohanness looks at his shoes, ashamed, smiles.

Stavros: "Here!"

He pulls off his own shoes and throws them at the boy's feet. Then, without another word, he turns and takes off. After a few steps, he stops and turns over his shoulder.

Stavros: "Where do you come from?"

Hohanness is frantically pulling on Stavros' shoes, fearful that he might change his mind.

Hohanness: "From far behind there. Behind those clouds are mountains, the mountains of Armenia. I won't ever see them again."

He jumps up, heartened by the gift. He tries out the shoes.

Hohanness: "Thank you. I'll remember you."

He turns west and walks directly into the setting sun.

⚜

In the Topouzoglou home, Stavros' family is at dinner. Seated on the floor around a low table are his four brothers and his three sisters, all younger than Stavros, two maiden aunts, and an old uncle. They pay no attention to anything except the food. Vasso is preparing a plate for Isaac, who is not in his place at the head of the table. She fills the plate and goes back and enters their bedroom. The family eats. They hear Vasso's voice.

Vasso: "Isaac, I have brought you some food."

All stop eating for a moment and listen. They hear no answer from Isaac. They shake their heads and cluck. Then they resume eating.

Vasso's voice: "Isaac! Now I want you to eat something."

Old Uncle: "He did this once before. Stayed in there for nine days."

Again, all stop eating and consider the gravity of the situation, making tstststtttssst sounds. Then back to their food.

In the parents' bedroom Isaac is sitting in a dark corner, his back to the door and to the room. Vasso makes a last effort.

Vasso: "Isaac!"

Isaac, finally, gravely: "Vasso, you are forgetting who you are and who I am. If I want food I will call you." Then sternly, but gently; "I don't want to see you now. I want to see my son."

Vasso exits without another word.

She comes to the table and puts down the plate of food. The boys immediately divide it among themselves.

Vasso: "He has something in his mind . . . something deep."

The door to the outside opens. They all turn.

Vasso: "So . . . at last . . ."

In the bedroom, Isaac has also heard the door open.

Isaac, a sudden cry: "Stavros!!"

He waits. After an instant, the boy comes in, followed by a demonic Vasso.

Issac: "I've been waiting for you."

Vasso, a fury: "Where are your shoes. What did you do with your shoes???"

Isaac: "Vasso!"

Vasso: "Well? Well ? What? Where?"

Isaac: "Vasso! Leave . . . now!"

Vasso, after a moment: "Yes, Isaac." Then, quietly to Stavros: "Remember! You're speaking to your father!"

She leaves. Father and son are alone.

Isaac: "Come here, boy. Sit here, close to me. When I don't see you for a day, you look changed. Will you have a coffee?"

Stavros: "No thank you, father."

Vasso comes back, carrying a pair of bedroom slippers. She kneels at Stavros' feet and puts them on him.

Isaac: "You'll have a coffee with me."

Vasso: "Tststtttssstttsst . . ."

Isaac: "Vasso, two coffees immediately."

Vasso: "Immediately."

She gets up and goes. Isaac's tone becomes intimate.

Isaac: "I have made up my mind."

Stavros: "Yes, father?"

Isaac: "We are going to send you to Constantinople."

Stavros: "What did you say, father?"

Isaac: "Our family is going to leave this place. You will go first."

Stavros gets up slowly and moves towards Isaac.

Isaac: "You will take with you everything this family has of worth."

Stavros kneels and takes his father's hand as if it were a holy object, bends over and kisses it.

Isaac, trying to go on: "You will take with you . . ."

He cannot continue. He is very touched by his son's expression of love for him.

Isaac: "You will . . . I said . . . everything of worth this family has."

Vasso and her eldest daughter, sixteen-year-old Athena, are in an upstairs bedroom. The girl has been working—when her household duties permit—on a hope chest to take to her husband when the day comes. Most of this dowry consists of small handcraft objects. One corner of her bedroom is filled with a small loom. Athena is on her knees taking a blanket off the frame. it is rather inexpertly woven, but it is dear to the girl. She rises and goes to Vasso and gives it to her, then brings up a couple more from a neat pile under the loom.

Vasso comforts the girl: "This winter I will come here at night and we'll weave together. By the day of your wedding you will have all the blankets you need."

In another bedroom, the youngest girl, Fofo, thirteen, is at the mirror, slowly removing her earrings. Her eyes are filled with tears. She has not taken these earrings off since the day her ears were pierced. Vasso enters, crosses to her, waits for an instant. Fofo gives her the earrings. Vasso kisses her and exits.

In the far corner of the cellar, Stavros and Isaac are on their knees, Isaac holding an oil lamp, Stavros digging with a small pick.

Isaac: "From time to time, I've had to do things that—well—we live by the mercy of the Turk. But, Stavros, I have always kept my honor safe inside me. Safe inside me! And, you see, we're still living. After a time you don't feel the shame."

In a corner of a back bedroom, the two aunts are giving up their wealth.

Vasso: "Anna, what will you do with them, little dearie, make yourself pretty? It's too late little dearie, it's too late."

She takes the lace collars. The aunt breaks into tears.

Stavros is still digging in the corner of the cellar. Isaac takes a letter out of his pocket.

Isaac: "So yesterday I had this back from Our Cousin in Constantinople." He reads: "'Beloved Isaac: I will be honored. Let Stavros bring money to put in my business and I'll make him my partner.' You know he has a prospering establishment there, you'll see a prospering . . ."

Stavros: "But father . . . will it be better for us in Constantinople . . . ?"

Isaac: "Yes! It will be!" Then, "Where can we go? It's our last hope."

It is not *Stavros'* last hope. He resumes digging.

Outside the main house is a small outbuilding where the family smokes its meat. Vasso and two of the brothers wrap slabs of this "Bastourma" in cloths.

One of the Brothers: "What are we going to eat this winter?"

Vasso: "When didn't you eat, fatty?"

The Other Brother: "The Chinese eat dog meat."

In the corner of the cellar, Stavros is still at work.

Isaac: "You will take with you all our smoked meat. You will take the two rugs on the floor upstairs. In fact everything you can sell, our donkey, you will take our donkey, Goochook, and sell him when you get to Constantinople. You will take the jewelry in this box."

Just then the pick hits the top of the box. Stavros and his father begin to pull it up.

Isaac: "The jewelry which came with Vasso when I took her for a wife."

ʊʊʊ

Upstairs, the family has gathered around the box which Isaac is opening. As the top comes off . . .

All: "Oh! . . . Oh!! Oh!!!"

Vasso pulls up a gold chain and locket.

Vasso: "This was my mother's. See! She's wearing it there . . ."

She points to an old picture hung on the wall. Its subject is a woman dressed in the style of the early nineteenth century. Vasso's mother was a proud woman with rather Mongoloid features. She is wearing the chain and locket.

Vasso: "I was going to give it to you when you got married."

She turns and looks at Stavros.

Athena: "It's better this way, mother."

On the eve of Stavros' departure the family gathers with greater formality. Isaac is conducting an historic meeting.

Isaac: "In time you will bring your three sisters to Constantinople. As the eldest, it is your responsibility to see that they marry well."

Stavros looks at his sisters solemnly. The girls look especially plain. Stavros smiles uncertainly.

Isaac: "Then in time, as your business prospers, you will bring your four brothers out and to your side. As the eldest it is your responsibility to set them up in business."

Stavros looks solemnly at his brothers.

Isaac: "Then it will be your mother's turn. It is your responsibility to make her final days happy ones."

Vasso: "Isaac, let's not ask too much!"

Isaac: "Vasso, there's a right way and a wrong way."

Vasso: "Yes, Isaac."

They both look at their eldest. The full load of responsibility is now on Stavros' back.

Later, with the ikons and candles prominent, the family sits, heads bowed, at prayer. But Vasso sits apart from them, sewing furiously on Stavros' coat.

Isaac: "My God, King Christ, gentle Lord Jesus, Who rose from the dead to look after mankind. We now commit our eldest son to Your loving care. Watch over him. He is our hope."

Vasso moves over close to Stavros.

Vasso, a heavy whisper: "Did you hear that?"

Stavros: "Yes."

Vasso: "He's trusting you with everything this family has. You realize that???!!!"

Isaac, sharply: "Vasso!!"

Vasso: "Forgive me, Isaac."

She resumes her sewing in silence.

Isaac: "Gentle, Holy Child, teach him that the meek shall inherit the earth."

The old uncle sneaks over to Stavros' side.

Old Uncle, whispering: "Except in this country!"

Isaac, aware of this interruption, is unable to bring himself to scold the old man. He simply waits.

Then Isaac continues: "Teach him that all men are brothers!"

Old Uncle: "Nevertheless, trust no one!"

Isaac: "That a gentle word and a Christian smile will turn away wrath."

Vasso comes alongside Stavros with the coat.

Vasso: "I have sewn the money into the lining. Feel it? Here! And in this little sack—the jewelry. Keep this coat on at all times. Are you listening? Even when you sleep."

Old Uncle: "Sleep with one eye open."

The uncle illustrates, closing one eye, waggling the other from side to side, pointing also with his finger from side to side.

This time Isaac speaks with all his authority.

Isaac: "Vasso! Be silent!"

Vasso drops her head. Then suddenly turns it away as an emotion overwhelms her. Isaac now speaks to her, more gently.

Isaac: "Vasso . . . what is it?"

Vasso: "My God! If you send him to the baker to bring bread you're never sure he'll come back. And now—Constantinople!! Look at him! Look at him!"

She begins to sob bitterly. The family has never before seen this woman cry. The children are awe-struck.

Isaac waits out her bitter sobs. Then he speaks, offering no comfort, only the truth as he sees it.

Isaac: "Vasso, if you and I have so brought up our eldest son that at this moment he can fail his family, we deserve to go down."

All turn now and look at Stavros. He sits there, the entire burden on his back. Then he gets up and goes to his mother, standing now awkwardly before her. He speaks, meaning it with all his heart.

Stavros: "I won't fail you."

Suddenly the mother and son embrace, she finally accepting him in his new position as head of the family.

A cluster of people, the Topouzoglou family, stands on a little mound, looking out at the vast Anatolian plain. Far, far in the distance, just mounting the first swell of the prairie, are two tiny figures, the boy, Stavros, and his heavily laden little donkey. At the crest he stops and turns. The boy is dressed in the coat his mother prepared for him. Under it, he wears a wing collar and tie. On his head is Vartan's fez. Now he waves goodbye. Then he turns his back on his family and speaks sharply to Goochook.

Stavros: "Come on you! Let's go you!"

He and the donkey go over the crest and are almost out of sight.

The family has seen him for what may be the last time. They turn and head back toward their city. The boy and his donkey are the tiniest figures on the vast plateau. Behind them, the sun sets.

2

The Kizzil is not a big river as rivers go, but it is the largest one in this part of the world. Stavros and Goochook are being ferried across it on a flat-bottomed boat. The ferryman works a single sweep.

The ferryman lays down his oar and the boat begins to drift in midstream. Stavros looks back nervously. So does Goochook. The ferryman begins to rock the boat vigorously. Stavros lets out a cry of fear. Country boys from the interior cannot swim. And the donkey, under his heavy load, would certainly not have a chance. Goochook begins to bray.

Stavros: "What are you doing?? You?? You?? I don't swim—YOU! What are you doing??? Allah!!"

The ferryman rocks the boat. The donkey panics.

Stavros: "Look out! The donkey! What do you want? I'll give you whatever you want. I'll give you more money!"

The ferryman immediately moves toward Stavros with his hand outstretched. Stavros hesitates. He looks at the distant shore, then at his overloaded donkey. He considers. Then he takes out a change purse which holds his small money. The moment the purse comes into view, the ferryman snatches it and takes all of its contents.

Stavros: "God will punish you."

Ferryman: "God knows my particular problems." He returns the empty purse. "Be grateful I'm not looking into what's on the donkey's back."

Even before the boat touches shore, the ferryman leaps off and runs. Stavros is hard after him. But behind him, the boat drifts from shore and the donkey begins to bray. Stavros has to run back. He shouts to the world in general, "Thief! Thief!"

As if in answer, a large swarthy Turk rises from under some rocks. Holding onto the boat, Stavros shouts. "Catch him! Catch him!" The ferryman's path of flight takes him past Abdul, the Turk. Abdul seizes him.

Abdul is large and the ferryman small. Abdul has him by the collar and is shaking him, dragging him back to Stavros.

Abdul: "Oh you mother-seller!" He calls out to Stavros: "I have him. Don't worry. I have him."

Later that day, Abdul and Stavros are on the road to Ankara. Stavros is walking behind Goochook. Abdul, a man without baggage, rides his own animal, his long legs extended, heels scraping the dust. He carries a cane. He is swarthy, in his mid-thirties, weighs two hundred odd pounds, and is a psychological enigma.

Stavros: "How will I ever thank you?"

Abdul: "It is I who am fortunate. After all, this road to Ankara is the home of every mother-selling bandit bastard in Turkey. What good fortune is mine to meet a brother on the road! Brother!"

He rubs the sides of his forefingers together, a gesture he is to repeat many times.

Stavros: "I beg you. It is my good fortune not yours."

Abdul: "You have such a sweet smile!" He speaks with passion. "You and I! Brothers!" Once again he rubs his forefingers together. "Anything I have is yours, just as I know that everything you have is mine."

Stavros gives him a sharp look. But Abdul is so open and so brotherly that Stavros' suspicion is laid to rest.

Time passes. It is midday and very hot. All

are weary. Goochook stumbles a little. Abdul stops.

Abdul: "Brother, my heart aches when I see that animal of yours struggle under the load you have put on his little back. I'm sure that, at this very moment, Allah, who sees all, is saying to himself: When will that good man who's always smiling"—Stavros stops smiling—"finally become aware of the pain he's causing that dear little beast? Do you think that is possible, brother?"

Stavros: "No. I mean . . . yes . . . yes . . . I suppose . . ."

Abdul: "Then, much as he'll balk, we must insist that my animal share the burden."

Stavros: "Oh, no!"

Abdul: "I insist. That smoked meat is heavy."

Stavros: "But then you'd have to walk too."

Abdul: "So!?" He dismounts quickly. "Come! Since we are brothers of the road, our animals must be brothers as well. Here. Help me."

He starts to untie the ropes which hold Goochook's burden.

Both donkeys are now burdened. They go on.

Later, as the sun sets, they stop on a hill overlooking the town of Mucur.

Abdul: "My brother, I know that town well. I have been the helpless victim of many a bandit in the town of Mucur. We'll camp here tonight on this hill."

Stavros: "If you advise. But what will we do for food?"

Abdul can't help looking at the smoked meat. Stavros notices.

Abdul: "I know what you're thinking. But I won't allow you to do it. I'd rather go hungry. Word of honor!"

They make a roadside camp and build a fire. Abdul eats heartily of the smoked meat with the greatest appreciation of its savor. Stavros watches him.

Abdul: "Eat, brother, eat. Food is strength. We have nine, ten days long journey to Ankara. And then . . . you go on?"

Stavros: "To Constantinople. Our cousin has a prospering rug establishment there."

Abdul's mind has moved on to another interest: "I notice you didn't remove your coat all day. Aren't you hot?"

Stavros: "Well . . . no . . . a little . . ."

He starts to take his coat off then doesn't. Abdul smiles, rubs his forefingers together, winks.

The heat of the midday sun beats down on the

road to Ankara like a huge fist. The men are dusty and weary as they trudge up a rocky hill. Abdul stops.

Abdul: "I can go no further."

He sits down and pulls off one shoe painfully.

Abdul: "They say the Prophet walked barefoot, but it must have been over different roads than these. Look!"

He puts a finger through a hole in the sole of his shoe.

Abdul: "I thought this damned pair of shoes would last the journey. But then I expected to ride the entire way. I wasn't prepared for all this walking. What do you think?"

Stavros: "Well . . ."

Abdul: "Oh, no! Oh my God, no! I see that look on your face: 'Abdul, the son of Abdul, is going to be a burden to me!' I would rather stay rooted to this spot for the rest of my life, word of honor!"

At a shoemaker's in the marketplace of the next town, Kursehir, Abdul is trying on a pair of new shoes. It is a rather flashy pair, not ideal for a long journey by foot over rough terrain. Abdul is berating the proprietor as Stavros stands by helplessly.

Abdul: "Aren't you ashamed! You would rob your mother! Just consider one thing, I beg you, my brother here has sold a side of smoked meat, one of the delicious pieces that his family entrusted to . . ."

Proprietor: "That is the price!"

Abdul turns to Stavros: "I've done my best!!"

Stavros doesn't answer. He wishes he had never hooked up with this man. After a moment he reaches into his pocket.

They are again on the road to Ankara. The day is hot. The road is hard under foot. Abdul is limping. Stavros is trying desperately to find a way to lose this man.

Stavros: "How are the new shoes?"

Abdul: "They pinch! My feet are covered with boils and sores."

Stavros: "Perhaps you should stay in the next town for a few days and rest?"

Abdul: "Oh? And you?"

Stavros: "I would go on."

Abdul: "Oh, no! I couldn't leave my brother. Don't fear. I'll never abandon you."

He limps along. Then stops abruptly, dramatically.

Abdul: "But brother, I must have a drink. My heart is dry! My spirit thirsts! One swallow of raki I must have!! You could not deny me one drink?"

Stavros and Abdul sit at a table in an outdoor cafe in Zordagh, a juncture point for camel and mule traffic. Here are ample provisions for everything that a mule or camel driver might look for after a week's journey over the burning plateau. It is a wild town.

Abdul is getting drunk. Stavros, his victim, watches him, still looking for a way to escape. A thunderstorm can be heard approaching. A waiter brings Abdul another raki.

Abdul: "Brother, I confess I cannot pay for this one."

Stavros: "You didn't pay for the others!"

Abdul: "Brother, it is not necessary to remind me that at this time I am less fortunate than you. After all, in friendship, there is only one rule. What is mine is yours and what is . . ."

Stavros, bursting: "But you have nothing!"

Abdul is patient with him: "As the Prophet said: 'Who can place a price on wisdom?' "

Stavros: "Despite the Prophet, this is the last I pay for."

Stavros becomes tense and silent. Abdul tries to get his attention. He rubs the sides of his forefingers together flirtatiously. He gets no response. Then Abdul bursts into tears.

Stavros: "What is the matter now???"

Abdul: "You wish you had never met me. Admit it. Admit it." Stavros will not respond. "For some reason you cannot speak what is obvious. Well . . . I had hoped to have my brother with me for the entire journey. Only last week a man was murdered between here and Ankara. As a matter of fact, not far from this town on the road to Ankara."

He drinks. Suddenly the rain comes down hard.

Abdul: "Behold! Allah weeps for me!"

It is a cloudburst. The two men run to find shelter for their donkeys.

They find an inn and secure their beasts in a low shed. The rain is beating down hard. Stavros runs into the inn. Abdul makes as if to follow, then runs back to the donkeys. He rips off the pack on Goochook and heads off in an opposite direction.

Later, inside the inn, Stavros sits at a window, alone, watching the rain, waiting. Abdul enters with two women. He holds a bottle. The women are plump, decidedly hirsute. With them is a small bear on a chain. They have all had—including the bear—a good deal to drink.

Abdul: "Brother, I have decided not to leave

you!" Stavros glares at him. "You don't seem to be as happy about this as I am. Where is your famous smile??" Stavros doesn't answer. "A confession! I sold the rest of the meat."

Stavros: "You sold the—!"

Abdul: "I did it for you! I swear. There is a saying, 'The rope drawn too tight will snap.' So behold, Chingana!" A flourish towards one of the women. "Chingana is yours! I don't know this other beast's name. But we will find out the facts about her before too long. The bear, I believe is also female." He bursts into song, dances. The bear dances.

"Oh pity the man without a woman.
   Aman!
Pity the man without a mate.
   Aman, aman!
A garden without water.
A meal without wine.
The sky without the moon.
The face without the eyes.
   Aman!"

Something snaps in the boy. He throws himself at Abdul. There ensues a quick and decisive engagement. Abdul knocks him cold with the back of a chair. Then he contemplates his victim with generous pity.

Abdul: "Poor thing, poor thing. Come, Chingana, take his legs. He's a good soul, a good boy. Come."

All three carry the boy upstairs.

Later, in a bedroom upstairs at the inn, Abdul and Chingana, drunk, are shaking Stavros.

Abdul: "Brother, brother. Don't worry! You are asleep but I am awake. I am looking after your precious possessions. I have brought them up out of the rain."

Stavros wakes up with a vengeance.

Stavros: "Allah!"

He leaps up and starts to look around.

Abdul: "They are all here. Every beautiful item!"

Stavros: "My sister's blankets, where are they?"

At this moment the woman Abdul calls "the Beast" makes an entrance from an adjoining room, clothed only in one of Athena's hope-chest blankets. She does a little belly dance.

Stavros is horrified: "What are you doing!!"

Abdul grabs "the Beast" and holds her lovingly, squeezing her soft parts.

Abdul: "Brother, while you were asleep, this woman has given me unspeakable pleasure. Ach! Ach! Aman!"

"The Beast" is drunk. Her hair is in disarray, her long yellow teeth glistening, her eyes bloodshot. She sways seductively, with only the blanket around her, trying her best to be ladylike at the same time.

Stavros is frantic, furious: "Where is my coat??"

They all burst out laughing.

Abdul: "You are wearing it, brother."

Stavros feels through the lining quickly. Abdul is really hurt.

Abdul: "You insult my father, brother, when you do that, you insult my father who taught me right from wrong. I am a patient man, brother, but you insult my mother, poor thing, long dead."

Abdul begins to blubber. Stavros is gathering his possessions.

Abdul: "But I forgive you! Now just look here. I can understand that this person must look to you like a beast. But do not go by her appearance. Penetrate to her soul. Take her into the other room."

He suddenly leaps up and grabs Stavros in a bear-like embrace.

Abdul: "I have never met a more generous

and brotherly person than you. This trip has been a landmark in my life."

He starts to kiss Stavros violently. Stavros shoves the drunken man away.

Stavros: "Where is my other rug? The small one?"

Abdul, hurt: "Brother, I beg you, don't use that tone of voice with me!"

Stavros: "Never mind my tone of voice. Where is my mother's little rug?!"

He throws himself at Abdul, clutching him by the neck. Abdul, shaky with drink and weak from love-making, cannot defend himself. The women scream.

Stavros: "You animal! Where is my mother's little rug???"

Now in rushes the proprietor of this miserable inn, and, following him, a hamal (a porter) and a couple of camel-drivers from across the hall. They pull Stavros off Abdul, but the boy keeps calling out.

Stavros: "Where is my mother's rug?"

Abdul points to the proprietor: "I gave it to him."

Stavros: "To him? You gave my rug to him! What for? What for?"

He turns on the proprietor. This is a tough man. He has to be to run a place like this. He shouts his own outrage.

Proprietor: "What? What for?!"

Abdul now has to restrain the proprietor from attacking the boy. Meantime he is admonishing Stavros.

Abdul: "Brother, brother . . . shshsh . . . brother! Courtesy! Reason!"

Proprietor: "What for? To pay for your night's lodgings. What for!"

Abdul turns to the proprietor: "Shshh! We're all gentlemen here." Then to Stavros: "Brother, I am at fault in this."

Stavros: "Give me my rug."

Proprietor: "Then pay for your room in cash money. What do you think the rug is anyway? A silk Keshan? It is a rag that I'm ashamed to have my friends see, so I put it on the floor of the toilet to soak up droppings."

During this speech, Stavros has been frantically gathering up the rest of his possessions. Abdul falls on his knees before him.

Abdul: "Brother, only I am at fault here. I beg your forgiveness. I cannot live without your forgiveness."

He tries to clasp Stavros around the knees, but the boy dodges him and continues to bundle up his possessions.

Abdul: "Before all this company, I beg for your forgiveness. Brother, don't leave me here on my knees! Don't insult my soul!"

Suddenly, Abdul's voice has a new note in it.

Abdul: "Brother, I have never before been on my knees before a Greek!"

Stavros pays no attention, starts out with his belongings.

Abdul, still on his knees: "Brother, I warn you! With a Turk there can either be brotherliness or its opposite. I warn you."

Stavros is gone. Abdul gets up slowly and dusts off his knees. He is suddenly cold sober.

Abdul: "Too bad! Ach, Ach, Ach! Too bad. So! Now!"

He looks demonic. He has been telling the truth: he did like the boy—and he has been mortally insulted. He rubs his forefingers together, sardonically, then draws one finger across his throat.

The next day. The sun is shining. Stavros and Goochook have walked all night on the road to Ankara and are exhausted. There is a single railroad track along the road. A very small train passes by. Stavros doesn't look up.

From a window of the train, Abdul has spotted his victim.

Late that afternoon Stavros and Goochook are coming into the outskirts of a town called Soosehir. Stavros, half asleep as he walks, looks up and sees two uniformed men—rural police—watching him.

Stavros, driving Goochook before him, passes by the police. Suddenly, they move in on him. He struggles a little, but his protests are useless. They drag him off.

Stavros: "What for? What for??!! What did I do???"

The process of justice in this town is conducted in a dusty and very shabby room in the judge's home. The judge sits cross-legged on the floor behind a low table. A familiar voice is heard.

Abdul stands there, the very picture of outraged justice.

Abdul: "Your honor, I made an exact list of every particular."

Stavros, between his guards, screams out: "Lies! Lies! Lies!" The rural policeman who is standing next to him backhands him across the mouth and knocks him off his feet: "Sssutt! Thief!" The judge gives the incident only the most perfunctory attention. He turns to a shabby clerk who holds Abdul's inventory.

Judge: "Read!"

The clerk reads. As each item is particularized, the policeman checks it.

Clerk: "One Hamedan carpet. The color of roses and the blue of midnight. A corner well worn."

Abdul: "Behold!"

Policeman: "As described."

Judge, half to himself: "Beautiful rug!"

Policeman: "One blanket, the color of peaches, woven at home by my dear sisters."

Abdul looks at Stavros indignantly. Stavros is standing with his head bowed, half turned away. No one there can see that he has opened the lining of his coat and is quickly swallowing coin after coin after coin.

Clerk: "Then! In the lining of the coat."

Stavros stops swallowing.

Abdul: "Your honor, make him take my coat off."

Judge: "Take off the coat."

It is a windy day. Stavros, without a coat, without donkey, without possessions of any kind is walking slowly into the low sun on the road to Ankara. He looks back and sees Abdul coming up, riding Goochook at a trot. Stavros' hand goes to his dagger, stays there.

The donkey catches up to Stavros. Abdul, riding alongside, addresses his victim in a friendly, chatty tone.

Abdul: "After you left I had a terrible time. Those policemen are not honest. And the judge! Aman! Aman! He offered to divide my new possessions with me. And then, when I declined, they all helped themselves. The judge particularly wanted the rugs. The law in this country needs considerable reform." Stavros does not answer. "Look! I'll show you what I have left!"

He holds out his hand with the sister's earrings, the locket, and a single coin. Stavros, his hand still on his dagger, doesn't turn his head.

Abdul: "Nothing! You see! Nothing!" No answer. "But there are some coins missing. About six of them by my estimate. I came to the conclusion you had swallowed them. No? I saw you do it. At the time I thought to myself, let him have something, poor thing. But now the situation had changed." He holds out his hand again. "You see! I cannot be so generous." No answer. "I admit you've been patient with me. If I had been you, I would long since have taken out the blade you hold there and put it to its proper use. But we Turks are primitive, while you Greeks are civilized. I envy you. You have learned how to bear misfortune, swallow insult and indignity, and still smile. I truly envy you." He looks at him, appraisingly. "Well . . . the coins? Eh? Anything happening yet? Not yet, eh? How long do you suppose?? God knows, eh? Eh? So . . . a drink?"

Stavros makes no sign of having heard. Abdul lifts his bottle and takes a long, long swig.

ʊʊʊ

It is sunset. Stavros sits with his back to some wild rocks. Abdul sits in the foreground, now quite drunk and completely unmasked.

Abdul: "You're really such a coward! Imagine what I would have done in your place!"

Stavros' face burns with shame.

Abdul: "All you can do is smile and swallow. Just a bag of guts. I've killed men like you and it's no different than killing a sheep. One clean cut almost anywhere and the life flows out. A twitch or two and it's over. Have a drink! No! Of course! You don't drink. You don't fight. You've no use for women. What kind of a man are you?" He yawns, stretches. "Well I can't waste more time over you. Unfortunately I haven't a weapon. I'll have to borrow your knife. No? Yes? What? Why don't you say something? Are you afraid to talk? Do you value your life? I don't know what you people are? Are you different from sheep? They won't fight for their lives either. It's getting dark. It's almost time for our game. Well I'll give you a few minutes. I'll do my evening prayer. And then."

Abdul gets up, spreads his prayer rug, and begins his ritual of prayer. Stavros knows it's now or never. His hand is on the dagger.

As Abdul kneels and bends to pray, Stavros, with the speed of youth, is on Abdul's back, driving the dagger home again and again. Abdul lets out a terrible cry. Goochook, startled, bolts.

Stavros stands up, trembling. He looks around furtively to see if there were any witnesses.

The donkey is galloping away as if it were running for its life.

Stavros, calling frantically: "Goochook!! Goochook!!"

Stavros sees his donkey disappear for good behind a rise. The little animal's panic communicates itself to him. He starts to run. Then he stops, turns, walks back toward the body of the man he's killed. Something is beginning to toughen in the boy. He bends over and goes through the dead man's pockets. He takes his jewels and all the money he can find, straightens, looks at the coins in his hand. He makes a sound: pain, anger? Disgust at himself. Then he puts the money into his pocket and walks off. Without knowing it he has resolved that this will never happen to him again.

Finally, wearily, Stavros reaches the ancient, huge, crumbling stone gate at the entrance to what was the citadel of Ankara. Here is a watering place for donkeys and camels. Also a market with the usual flamboyant peddlars and the legion of beggars with their spectacular ailments. Through the arch can be seen the setting of the sun.

Stavros, covered with dust, is older looking, tougher.

He finds the railroad station. The sign reads: ANKARA. The boy takes out his remaining funds, a palm full of small coins. Then he makes up his mind and approaches the ticket window. There is a poster of the North German Lloyd Line advertising passage to America. It shows a steamboat going by the Statue of Liberty. Stavros looks at this for an instant, then he says to the ticket vendor, "Constantinople!" He puts his entire wealth on the ticket counter.

Stavros has arrived in Constantinople. He gazes in wonder at the six minarets of Santa Sophia. Soon we find him taking in the Golden Horn, the famous inside harbor of Constantinople. It is the busiest place in the city during the day. He watches the ferryboats in the harbor, the little water taxis, then he hears the sound of a big boat—a heavy steam whistle. His head jerks around. A large cargo ship is loading at a dock. An endless line of porters, at least one hundred men, go in, come out of the ship's hold.

Stavros hurries toward the ship. Then he looks up. The ship is flying the American flag.

Some American officers are supervising the loading from the rail of the cargo ship. They have open, decent faces. Stavros suddenly begins to call out.

Stavros: "America . . . America . . . eh? Eh, eh?"

The officers at the rail pay no attention to him. They're looking at the line of hamals loading the ship. A man, too old for his burden, buckles and falls. His burden falls to one side. Three men on the dock start for it.

Stavros, almost on instinct, unexpectedly even to himself, also goes after the load and the job. There is a terrible fight. All four men desperately want the job. Stavros fights like a wild beast. All his pent-up anger explodes. He lays about him with fury. In a few decisive seconds, he has the fallen man's load and his job. He snarls as he hoists it up on his back, then triumphantly starts up the gangplank.

The American officers have been watching the fight. As Stavros goes past the officers, he carries his burden proudly.

Officer in Charge: "Hello, kid!!"

Stavros struts and whistles, makes faces, proud of winning, dancing off under his load. Three big blasts of the ship's whistle are heard, as if it too were celebrating Stavros' victory.

It is dawn when the freighter, fully loaded, heads out to sea. A couple of hundred yards from shore, the whistle sounds again three times, "Goodbye," from a distance.

The dock is empty now, except for a solitary figure. Stavros is watching the freighter go. He has touched his dream. And now—he turns sadly and goes off.

The "closed" bazaar is made up of street after street of small, tightly packed store fronts, "closed" because all of them are under a glass arcade. It is the popular hour for buying, so the place is fantastically crowded. Fiercely competing vendors fill the middle way, their goods spread on paper laid on the paving.

Stavros holds a slip of paper in his hand, asks a direction, is given instructions, and goes on. The noise is overwhelming.

Around a corner of the bazaar, everything is

suddenly much quieter. Here are the rug stores. Stavros consults the piece of paper in his hand. Then he walks along the front of a row of rug stores, reading their numbers and their names.

These stores are very quiet indeed. Stavros stops. He has found the Topouzoglou Persian Carpet Company. Stavros inspects the front of this small, dark store. The inside is quiet as a tomb. Stavros is disappointed. He expected a "prosperous establishment."

Stavros enters. Stops. No one comes up to him. Silence. Then the sound of a powerful rhythmic snore. Stavros looks for the source.

Our Cousin lies on top of a small pile of folded carpets, peacefully asleep. An old porter, wearing slippers, comes up to Stavros.

Stavros, with obvious disappointment: "Is this the establishment of Odysseus Topouzoglou?"

The Porter: "Yes. Welcome, welcome."

Then he takes a good look at the visitor and sees how bedraggled he is. His tone changes.

The Porter: "What do you want? We want nothing."

At this moment Our Cousin stirs, and then emits a marvelous variety of sighs, groans, and grumbles.

Our Cousin: "Ach! Ach! Ach! Tstststststststt! Tststst! Aaachh!"

Stavros: "What's he saying?"

The Porter: "He's forgiving God for bringing him into such a world."

Stavros: "I'm his cousin. When will he wake?"

The Porter: "When business comes." He looks at the floor, at Stavros' feet. "Look at the dirt you brought in here. Who'll have to sweep again? Me!"

At this moment something wakens Our Cousin. He looks around, smiling vaguely. His mouth is sour. He rubs his gums, goes "Ach, ach."

The Porter: "Topouzoglou, effendi. This man says he's your cousin."

It is a dark establishment, and the old man's eyes aren't too good. Also he naps with his glasses off. Now, as he approaches Stavros, he first chortles.

Our Cousin: "Oh, ohh, oooohhh, welcome, welcome."

His glasses on, he now takes a good look. And *his* tone of voice abruptly changes.

Our Cousin: "What happened to you?"

Stavros: "I . . . I had a bad journey."

Our Cousin: "Well, well, poor thing, poor thing!" He turns to the Porter. "Artin! Run, run, two coffees. Immediately!"

Artin, walking off slowly: "Immediately."

Our Cousin: "I've been waiting and waiting. Welcome! Here, come, come in the back of the store. I have clean linen. Then I'll buy you lunch."

Our Cousin takes Stavros to a restaurant overlooking the harbor. Fired with the dregs of his energy, he is putting on a good show. Stavros is ravenous, even eating the fish heads.

Our Cousin: "So, what we need is more stock."

From across the harbor, the sound of the whistle of a large boat. Stavros' head swings around, listening.

Our Cousin: "What?"

Stavros: "Forgive me. I was merely going to remark that you don't seem to be selling what you have."

Our Cousin: "You are very sharp! Another mullet? I beg you. They are so small!!"

Stavros, ravenous: "Since you insist, I will. Thank you."

Again the sound of the whistle of a large freight boat.

Our Cousin: "You see I have the wrong goods for the market as it is today."

Stavros hears only the whistle.

Back at the Topouzoglou Persian Carpet Company, Our Cousin is showing Stavros his stock of rugs and carpets.

Our Cousin: "What I will do, as soon as you know the business, is to take the money you have brought, go to Persia and buy the kind of goods that . . ." He notices Stavros' silence. "What is the matter, cousin?"

Stavros blurts it out: "I haven't brought any money."

Our Cousin: "You . . . ?"

Stavros: "I was a fool and I was robbed."

Our Cousin: "You're teasing me."

Stavros: "No. I'm ashamed to face you."

Our Cousin: "But your father——?"

Stavros: "I'm ashamed to say it."

At this moment Our Cousin seems to have a heart attack. He clutches his breast, moans, groans, and carries on.

Stavros: "Cousin . . . Cousin . . ."

Our Cousin, suddenly shouting: "Then why did you eat my lunch??!!"

Stavros: "I was hungry."

Our Cousin is shouting when he isn't groaning. "Go, go, go out of my sight." Stavros starts out. "No, no, don't go. Sit down. For God's sake, give me a chance to swallow this. Why did you eat my lunch? Two of everything! Two of everything! The day of my ruination!"

An hour later Stavros is sitting alone in the front of the store. Our Cousin approaches, carrying a broom.

Our Cousin: "Here! Ruination! Sweep!"

He hands him the broom and Stavros begins to sweep.

Our Cousin: "I will write your father. He's a good man and . . ."

Stavros drops the broom and rushes to Our Cousin.

Stavros: "No, listen, NO! He must never know what happened. Promise! Not a word. Promise."

Our Cousin: "I only meant to say that in time your father will . . ."

Stavros: "Do you want to kill him? He put everything on me . . . everything!!! It will kill him if . . . I am going to make it up to him. I have big plans. They will be proud of me. But now, now, nothing. Hear? Promise? Nothing!"

Our Cousin: "All right. I promise!" Then, "Go on. Sweep! My ruination! Sweep!"

Stavros starts again to sweep. Our Cousin walks to the window and looks out on to the street.

Stavros vows to himself: "They'll be proud of me!"

Our Cousin at the window, indicates the street: "Look! The rich come to work after lunch, in a carriage, while I . . ." Suddenly he seems to have an inspiration. "Stavros. Listen!" Stavros stops sweeping. "God is fertile! Behold!"

Outside in the street a carriage has drawn up in front of a large establishment. A prosperous, extremely well-fed rug merchant is getting out.

Our Cousin: "Behold Aleko Sinyosoglou! A man with a great deal of money, a very large stock, and four daughters, one plainer than the other, so much so that day by day he is losing hope of ever becoming a grandfather. You understand??"

Stavros: "No."

Our Cousin: "God solves all problems! We must not at this moment forget that you are a young man, even handsome, and if properly dressed . . . do you understand now?"

Stavros now does: "No." He turns away in complete disgust. "Allah!"

Our Cousin looks at the recalcitrant. Now he's peeved.

Our Cousin: "Never mind! You! Sweep! I'll arrange a meeting . . . and you'll see . . ."

Stavros begins to sweep. Then suddenly he

flings the broom away, almost hitting the porter who leaps from behind some rugs like an animal flushed from hiding. Without a word, Stavros exits from the store.

In the window of the office of the North German Lloyd Line, along with the usual posters and displays, is a model of the passenger liner *The Kaiser Wilhelm,* which makes the Constantinople-to-New York run.

Stavros strides into the office. At the counter the boy speaks to a clerk.

Stavros: "What do I need to go to America?"

The clerk looks down his nose at this frantic young man.

Clerk: "Money."

Stavros: "How much?"

Clerk: "You mean third class of course. One hundred and eight Turkish pounds."

This is to Stavros an astronomical figure.

Stavros: "One hundred and eight—! Allah!" Then, "All right."

The clerk looks at him scornfully and begins

to move away. Stavros reaches across the counter and holds him. With his free hand he points at the Assistant Manager.

Stavros: "Is he American?"

The Assistant Manager is very American. He wears a straw hat indoors, and is very much admired by some employees who work there. "Completely," says the clerk, speaking as of a god.

Stavros, his face pure jealousy and longing, takes in the American.

Stavros: "I'll be back."

And he exits from the office abruptly.

Back in Stavros' home, his family is at dinner. Isaac is reading a letter to the family—to Vasso, the children, the aunts, the old uncle.

Isaac: " 'And now I don't know where he is. At any rate he didn't bring me a single penny. Nothing! He says he was robbed. I tried to talk to him, Cousin, as is my place and duty. But suddenly he threw a broom at my porter and ran out of the store, his eyes on fire.' "

Vasso groans. The old uncle bursts out laughing.

Vasso: "What is amusing you, idiot?"

Isaac picks up another letter.

Isaac: "Now listen." He reads from the second letter. " 'Father, I couldn't trust our money to him. No one ever comes into his store. He sleeps all day on a pile of rugs. So I told him I was robbed. Meantime I have a new plan, a big idea! I'll have news for you very soon. I have already found another line of work. One that is much more active, in truth very active.' "

Vasso: "Well, that's good, anyway."

Old Uncle: "God knows what's going on."

Isaac: " 'My health is good. Tell mother that one way or another I get what I need to eat.' "

Vasso: "One thing he could always do."

Old Uncle: "Eat!"

Issaic: " 'So don't worry. One day you'll be proud of your son. That day will come, I promise you, you'll be proud of me!' "

3

Back in Constantinople, fifteen empty crates can be seen, one on top of another, jogging down a narrow, crowded street. If somewhere under them there is a man, we cannot see him.

Soon, however, it can be seen that it is Stavros who is carrying the crates. It is a hot summer's day and he is wringing wet and very worn.

In the shade of a warehouse, the hamals, or porters, are eating lunch. Stavros, who has no lunch, watches the others eat. One of the hamals, Garabet, has had enough of his bread and starts to throw it away.

Stavros, quickly: "Don't throw that away!"

He grabs it and wolfs it down.

Garabet: "Why don't you spend a few coins for a bread?"

Stavros smiles. But there is something manic about his smile now.

Behind a restaurant. Night, early Fall. Stavros and a couple of poor people have been waiting for the garbage to be put out. As soon as it is, they begin to pick it over. A dog tries to get in there, but Stavros drives him off.

Garabet watches him. He is an intellectual among hamals, a man \of fifty, cynical, wise, sour, tough. Stavros fascinates him.

Garabet: "Say . . . you!"

He points.

Along the street comes a mother donkey followed by her newborn foal. Their owner goes into a doorway for a moment.

Garabet, mocking: "Milk!"

Stavros pulls a little battered tin cup free from his belt, and starts toward the mare.

Months have passed. It is a cold, rainy November. Stavros and Garabet are working. Garabet has attached himself to the boy now, and they work as a pair. Stavros is tough as leather.

It is the end of a long dark day, and time now for the hamals to be paid off. Some young whores wait nearby. Garabet catches Stavros looking at them longingly. One of the whores, passably attractive, looks at Stavros.

Garabet: "I'm cold. I need a woman tonight. Want to come?" Stavros shakes his head. "I'll pay for it." Stavros shakes his head again. "You need it."

Garabet makes a vulgar illustrative gesture. Stavros won't look.

Stavros: "I need nothing."

Garabet: "Did you ever have one?" Stavros shakes his head. "Don't you want one?"

Stavros: "My father wouldn't approve."

Garabet makes a vulgar gesture relative to Stavros' father. At that moment Stavros is paid and starts off.

Garabet: "Where are you going?"

Stavros: "I have another job."

Garabet: "Now? Another job? At night?" Stavros nods. "Here." He offers him his cargo-knife. "Kill yourself with this. It's easier!"

Stavros' night work is in the kitchen of a large restaurant, a noisy place, full of filthy steam. He is washing dishes. His face is white as soap. A kitchen maid, a child of fifteen, flirts with him. He sticks to his work. She gives up, eats something.

ʊʊʊ

It is dawn and snowing. In a low shed, the man-drawn carts used to carry produce from market to market are stacked one atop another. Garabet walks up to one of them. He reaches under some burlap and shakes someone. Stavros bolts upright, drawing his knife, a wild animal, ready for anything.

Stavros: "Oh. You. There are thieves everywhere here. Like cats! What time is it?"

Garabet: "Get up. It's the hour. They're working. Aren't you cold?" Stavros shakes him off. "Come sleep on my floor tonight." Stavros shakes him off. "You need a good night's sleep."

Stavros: "I need nothing."

Then with a sudden gaiety he leaps out of the cart.

Stavros: "Allah! Come on you! Let's go, old man!!"

Stavros and Garabet pull two of the carts through the snow, side by side.

Garabet: "How much for a ticket?"

Stavros: "One hundred and eight pounds."

Garbabet: "Aman! And by now you've brought together—?"

Stavros: "What do you care?"

Garabet: "How much?"

Stavros: "Four pounds and a little. So?"

Garabet: "So how long do you expect to live?"

Stavros doesn't answer, whistles madly. Garabet looks at him.

Garabet: "Your harness is coming apart."

The seasons change. There is a lemony sunshine in the market square. It is spring. A squabble is taking place. One of the hamals has rejected a load as too heavy. He throws it down.

Hamal: "That load is for an animal! Get an animal!"

The loader in charge looks for the man who never refuses a load.

Loader: "America! America!"

Stavros, sitting on the ground repairing his hamal's harness, hears himself called, stands, puts his hands and arms through the loops in the harness, hitches it up onto his back, and goes trotting off in the direction of the loader with little coolie steps. In his patchwork clothes, he has to run the gauntlet of the other hamals, who resent him for accepting loads they have refused. "America, America" has become his nickname and is now directed at him with scorn as he goes by.

Time passes. It is summer again. Garabet, in the marketplace, steals a melon from a passing cart. He walks to Stavros, who is sleeping in a mess of vegetable garbage. The boy hugs his hamal's harness, as if it were all he had in the world. His face, in the sunlight, is pale and worn. He is on the verge of final exhaustion.

Garabet looks down at the boy and puts the point of his shoe in a delicate spot, wiggles it. Stavros awakens with a jolt. He seems overwrought.

Stavros, frantically: "What time is it?"

Garabet: "You have time."

He breaks the melon and offers part of it to Stavros.

Stavros: "I can't stay awake! I keep falling asleep."

Garabet: "Don't worry. You'll be dead soon." He raps Stavros' middle. "What's the baby weigh now?"

Stavros: "What? Oh. Seven pounds and a little."

Garabet, devouring his piece of melon: "Small money! There are two kinds of money. Small money and big money. Small money is a whore. Look at a coin. She's been in everyone's hands. You wake in the morning, she's gone. Now then, there's big money. Like what you need . . ."

Stavros had fallen asleep again. Garabet takes the other piece of melon from his limp hand and begins to eat it.

Stavros and Garabet are taking in the sunset over the busy harbor. The dock is a lovers' promenade. A pair of girls go by. Garabet notices Stavros looking at them with intense longing.

Garabet: "Behold! You're human!" Then he gets back to his favorite subject. "Now big money! Now big money is fertile! It procreates —how I don't know, but it reproduces itself. Every time you look—behold, more! There are only two ways for men like us to get big money. Steal it. Or if you're young, marry it. But you can't get it by work. Study me. Worked like an animal from the first day I could walk and carry! So? Behold! The lowest form of life."

He looks at Stavros, who is still watching the girls.

Garabet: "Oh! If I were you! There are some very ugly girls with very rich fathers!"

A couple of men pick the girls up. Stavros drops his head. In some odd way, he is disappointed.

Garabet: "Let's get ourselves a couple of those little mousetraps . . ."

He grabs Stavros in a vulgar mocking lover's embrace. Stavros pushes him off. Then Garabet speaks in simple friendship.

Garabet: "Come on, boy, you need it." And he shows him what he needs, wiggling his shoulders and so on.

Stavros: "I need nothing."

Garabet: "You need it! After work, come to my place. I'll have one there for you . . ."

Stavros hesitates, comes close to Garabet and whispers: "I . . . I've never . . . I wouldn't know—exactly—what to do."

Garabet: "Oh . . . they show you all that."

üü

Garabet's room is a hovel. The spill of light from the opening door reveals a young woman. We can't see her too well.

Stavros is at the door. His face is starved for human warmth.

Girl's Voice: "Yes, yes, come, close the door."

Stavros starts for her.

Afterward, Stavros lies on top of her in an absolutely dead sleep. Both are naked. A ragged burlap partially covers him. Nothing could wake him. He is in absolute exhaustion. She is not. She finds his money belt. Her fingers extract the coins, one by one.

In the market place at dawn, hamals are loading up for the day.

Loader: "America, America!"

Garabet looks around, but there is no sign of Stavros. A checker assigns Garabet his load. But he drops it and runs off. In the background we hear, "America, America!"

In Garabet's room, Stavros is ripping up everything in sight, looking for his money. Garabet enters.

Stavros: "Garabet!"

Garabet: "What happened?"

Stavros: "My money . . . the girl . . . where is she? I have to find her. Where do I . . . ?"

Garabet: "I don't know."

Stavros: "I have to find her. Nine months, nine months I worked! Where did *you* find her? Who is she?"

Garabet: "She's my daughter."

Stavros: "Your . . . ? Allah!"

Garabet: "Yes."

Stavros: "Well then, well then . . ."

Garabet: "I don't know where she is."

Stavros: "Well, how did you . . . ?"

Garabet: "I passed her on the street last night."

Stavros: "Where does she stay?"

Garabet: "Where they all stay, I suppose, there's a quarter."

Stavros: "Is this the way she lives—by selling herself?"

Garabet: "Are you a child? What else has she got to sell?"

Stavros: "Garabet! Garabet, I worked nine months!"

Garabet: "She did you a favor."

Stavros: "What?!"

Garabet: "I said she did you a favor!"

Stavros hits Garabet with all his might. Stavros is now very strong and hard-fisted. Garabet hits the wall, comes back, knife in hand, going for Stavros' throat, his free hand holding Stavros by the hair. He barely restrains himself. He's suspended for an instant, blind with rage just under control.

Garabet: "I should kill you. You know? I don't like you that much. You're not a boy, you know? You know? If you do that you have to be ready to go on. You know?" Then, challenging: "I said she did you a favor!" He waits. "Do you imagine you could have brought together one hundred and eight pounds the way you did the seven? That way? The human body—it hasn't that strength!" He glares at him. "I should really kill you." Then, "So. Come."

He starts out. Stavros follows.

>>>

Vartuhi is a whore. Her room is above a cabaret where Turkish cafe society comes to hear music and to dance. Her room is not large. But the bed, behind a curtain of beads, is. Vartuhi occupies it now with a customer. A single lamp burns oil.

The door bursts open and in comes Garabet, followed by Stavros. Garabet goes right to the bed and seizes his daughter. The customer jumps out of bed and begins to run from side to side, shrieking like a cornered chicken. Stavros stays by the door, blocking it. We cannot hear what Garabet says to his daughter, but it is all curses. He beats her. She screams.

Garabet: "Who did you give his money?"

Vartuhi: "Stop! The patron. Downstairs. Stop!"

He smacks her again. She screams.

Vartuhi: "He was going to put me out! On the street!"

Garabet drops her, starts out.

Garabet, to Stavros: "Come."

They exit.

Vartuhi runs to the door, calling after him: "You want me out on the street? Without a room and a bed, what am I? I'm an animal—without a bed and a room!"

The patron, a large bulky Turk, is at home in his quarters. He is entertaining two members of the Municipal Police in full uniform. They are all eating pastries, dripping honey over their chins, and drinking hot sweet tea out of small glasses. Garabet and Stavros have just come in.

Policeman: "If you go to whores, you must expect to be robbed."

Patron: "Your daughter! Three months she didn't pay!"

His wife—three hundred pounds—enters from the kitchen.

Wife: "She'll owe him again next week. Next week! He's the saint of patience with them, the saint of . . ."

The policeman suddenly makes a terrible sound: "Aahahahhhcchchhh! We were enjoying ourselves here." Then, with a violent gesture, "Go on . . . get out . . . go on before I . . . go on, get out!"

Garabet turns and puts it up to Stavros.

Garabet: "You want to say something?"

Stavros: "Allah!"

He walks out, beat! Garabet follows.

∿∿∿

In a corner on the waterfront Stavros finds a place to weep. Garabet, in his own way, is trying to comfort him.

Garabet: "I'm still angry you know." Then, gently: "I should still kill you. A fact! I should kill you!" The boy can't stop sobbing. "You hit me! Very hard! Very, very, very hard. You're a strong boy."

This doesn't work so he tries another tack.

Garabet: "You want to kill her? Go kill her. I won't stop you."

This doesn't do any good.

Garabet then speaks with gentle concern and real sympathy: "Anyway it's time for you to grow up and see the truth." He imitates him: " 'Big things' . . . 'Big things!' " And then, mockingly: " 'They're going to be proud of me.' "

Stavros yells with pain: "Don't do that!!"

Garabet, now cruelly mocking: " 'They're going to be proud of me! Some day they'll be proud of me!' Hah!"

Stavros: "They will be."

Garabet: "You're nothing now and you never will be!"

Stavros: "I will, I am, I will, I am, I will. I'm going to leave this place. There is a better place."

Garabet: "It's all the same. Tell me. Since you left home, have you met among Christians, one follower of Christ? Have you met among human beings, one human being?"

Stavros: "You!"

Garabet: "Me! Didn't you look in my face?? You don't know me. You don't know what I am . . ."

$$\text{Ψ Ψ Ψ}$$

In a cellar, a secret political group is being addressed by Garabet. He is one of the leaders of the underground. Stavros is in the audience.

Garabet: "I have one idea for this world. Destroy it and start over again. There's too much dirt for a broom. It calls for a fire. It needs the flood."

Another meeting. Another cellar. Another night. Many of the same men are there. And Stavros also. He seems exhausted, deeply discouraged, and here at this place only because he doesn't know where else to turn. The atmosphere in this second gathering is more conspiratorial. The conversation is in whispers. Attention is directed toward a door. They're waiting for someone.

Man: "I'll say this: the main victims of the Turkish Empire are the Turkish people. One day Turkey will be a great nation."

Stavros: "After I'm dead, I'm not interested."

Garabet explains, mocking the boy: "He still thinks there's a clean life somewhere, eh? America, eh?"

A ferocious-looking man—in some way crippled—comes out of a corner.

Cripple: "Don't tell me about America. I was there. I helped build one of their buildings."

He lifts his shirt, revealing a long, ugly scar.

Cripple: "I fell—and then? No one needed me. If you have money in America you're somebody. If you have no money, it's just like here. Life is for the rich!"

Garabet, speaking for Stavros, mocking: "He still thinks the same."

Stavros manages the faintest smile, the slightest nod.

It's not that he's lost sight of his objective. It's simply that he doesn't know, at the moment, how to go about reaching it. Suddenly everyone is silent. A man has entered, walks to the position of authority, and now speaks.

The Leader: "Anyone who's going to go, go now."

Garabet makes a little gesture suggesting to Stavros that he go. Stavros only sinks lower down in his chair. Behind them the door is locked. The meeting starts.

Later. A bomb is being concealed in a hamal's harness. The group around the bomb whispers.

The Leader: "Again! After the explosion, we separate. We meet one month from today. On the street you don't acknowledge each other. Is that clear?" All nod. Stavros nods.

At this instant the windows are suddenly filled with police and guns. The single oil lamp is shot out. Volley after volley. Screams of pain. The cries of the desperate. Then the shots stop. The door is broken in, admitting a kind of light. The smoke is settling. The carnage is terrible to behold. The dead in their last struggle. Then all is quiet, except for the final sounds of the dying.

In a military hospital, two army doctors are walking through a ward. They stop over a pallet and look down.

First Doctor: "It's too much. Look at him. A boy! All he wanted was something. What? Freedom. What?"

Second Doctor: "Shshsh!"

He indicates an orderly coming up. The tone of the First Doctor becomes traditionally autocratic.

First Doctor: "Here! You! You know when a man is dead?"

We see Stavros on the pallet. He is barely alive. A scar is burned into his forehead. He will never lose it.

Orderly: "I can tell when a mule is dead."

Doctor: "It's the same. With this one it's a matter of hours. There's a wagon full of them back of the kitchen. Go on—throw him in. He's finished."

The wagon of the dead is being driven through the countryside. The bodies are covered with a tarpaulin. Then one body, as if in a gentle slow-motion fall, emerges from under the tarpaulin and reaches the ground in the wake of the moving wagon, somehow, without a jar.

The body has life in it, but not much. A desperate effort and it reaches the side of the road.

Then Stavros rolls over into the ditch. The effort has exhausted him. He lies there, straining to breathe. A mongrel dog comes up.

⚊⚊⚊

A cliff by the sea, a sheer one hundred and fifty feet into the blue Sea of Marmor. Soldiers are throwing bodies over the precipice.

Garabet's body goes into the sparkling blue water, breaks through the kelp, rises, floats, then is engulfed. On the cliff, a few scattered people, Vartuhi among them, stand at a little distance from the soldiers. She turns, starts off.

⚊⚊⚊

The people on the road back to town see something, hesitate, then walk around and past it. The something is Stavros, trying to make his way back to town on his hands and knees. His head is bloody, his clothes indescribably disheveled. He falls, struggles up, falls.

He lies in the middle of the road, waiting for a few drops of strength to come back. Vartuhi's feet come into his view. She stoops and helps him up.

Back home, the Topouzoglou family sit in their garden under a vine. A letter has arrived with bad news.

Isaac, reading: " 'I don't know where to look further, dear Cousin, I have looked everywhere. He's disappeared from the face of this black world.' "

Isaac puts the letter down. The family sit in silence.

In Constantinople, Vartuhi's room is stifling hot. Her "patron" is at the door.

Patron: "If you're married, go elsewhere. We're in business, here."

Vartuhi: "But he doesn't stay here any more. He's gone."

Patron: "I can smell him!"

He walks into the room past her. And after an instant's search in the tiny room, he throws open the door to a small and shallow wardrobe. On the floor is Stavros. His eyes shine like those of a trapped wild animal. He is soaked with perspiration. One hand is out of sight.

Patron: "Now hear me. Tomorrow. Tomorrow I'm going to see some money from you. I haven't had a copper in three weeks. So tomorrow! Eh?! Final."

He walks out, the door shutting behind him.

We hear Stavros in a frantic whisper: "Ssst! Ssst! Vartuhi, come here!!"

Vartuhi comes to him, sitting on the floor. He seizes her arm with demonic strength. The hand that was concealed comes into sight. It holds his grandfather's knife.

Stavros: "Don't let him frighten you. I just

need a few more days. I'm getting my strength! My strength is coming back."

Vartuhi, thoroughly frightened: "Yes, yes."

Stavros gives her the knife: "Here, take this. Sell it and bring me food!"

Vartuhi: "Dear . . . dear little thing! Why don't you go home to your family??"

Stavros, an earthquake: "Go on. Get out. Bring me some pieces of meat! Some bread, some meat!!"

Vartuhi: "Yes, yes. Listen, do you think you're strong enough to take a walk this afternoon? The sun is shining. Go sit by the water this afternoon. When you come back, I'll have a little money. And piece by piece I'll pay you everything. I promised my father, and I promise you, everything."

Stavros: "Never mind that! I don't need small money now. I need a suit of clothes. A blue suit of clothes."

Vartuhi: "Well . . . I do have a friend . . . you know . . . an old man who comes here. He makes suits for men and . . ."

4

A Greek Orthodox church, Constantinople. The service is in progress. The men of the congregation stand in a body in the nave of the church. The women sit in a pew at the side. The service is sung. Stavros and Our Cousin enter, light candles, and stand among the other men. Stavros wears a blue suit and wing collar, and has not shaved his upper lip. He looks pale but very handsome.

Our Cousin, out of the side of his mouth: "Where did you get the beautiful suit??"

Stavros doesn't answer. There is something new, formidable about the boy! Ungiving! Our Cousin's attention goes to the Sinyosoglou family, a model of bourgeois prosperity. The five Sinyosoglou brothers are in their middle age and are all in business together. Here they are, on Sunday, standing in a line, their hands folded across their abdomens. Their women, sitting at the side, are indistinguishable one from another.

Our Cousin whispers to Stavros, points to the prosperous Sinyosoglou men. Stavros looks at the Sinyosoglou women, models of devout propriety. Then both he and Our Cousin look at a very plain young woman, with a long nose and a sallow face. Her name is Thomna. She is the heart of the matter. Stavros makes a sign of assent.

The men of the Sinyosoglou family have noticed Our Cousin's attention and also that of the young man with him. They nod. Our Cousin returns the nod. Then he nudges Stavros. Stavros now nods, proudly, even haughtily. Thomna Sinyosoglou gives Stavros one lightning glance. Then she drops her eyes demurely.

The living room of Aleko Sinyosoglou. Present are Aleko and his four brothers, and the guest of this occasion is Our Cousin. They are seated in a line. Each brother has the top button of his trousers unbuttoned and has so released his belly to protrude in comfort. Two women of an indefinite age are passing Turkish Delights, heavily dusted with sugar, and glasses of cool water on a tray to wash down the sweets.

A conference is in progress, which, despite its dulcet tone, is "strictly business."

Our Cousin: "He's the eldest son of the finest family in all that part of Anatolia. You must have heard of them: the Topouzoglous?"

Aleko, the father of the girl: "Yes, yes, of course. Nevertheless, there remains this question. Is his father able to bring with the boy a substantial amount of money?"

Our Cousin, after a tiny pause: "You're talking about money?"

Aleko: "That's something we must talk about."

Our Cousin: "We have questions, too."

Aleko: "But you know our business."

Our Cousin: "Still you have four daughters. There is the necessary division."

Aleko: "For each there will be enough. Now —I don't remember your telling me what business the boy is in."

Our Cousin: "Well . . ."

Our Cousin's game is to stall till Thomna meets Stavros. His hope is that when this happens, the matter of dowry and bilateral endowment will seem less important than the happiness of the two individuals whose fates are being discussed.

At the front window, some sons, cousins, whatnot, have been waiting for the arrival of Stavros. And now . . .

Boys: "He's here! He's here!"

The door to the kitchen swings open, and the opening is filled with the anxious faces of the Sinyosoglou women. Among them, Thomna.

Outside of the Sinyosoglou home, a carriage is releasing an elegantly dressed young man. Stavros pays the driver off with a flourish. He carries a cane.

Two of the plump brothers are at the window now. They turn from the impressive spectacle of Stavros stepping out of his carriage and nod approbation at Aleko.

In the kitchen Thomna's mother, her aunts, and her three younger sisters are fussing over her.

Anoola, her mother, speaks with a slight impediment: "Your figure looks very nice when you stand up straight and give it a chance."

Thomna: "Oh, mother, you're never going to be able to make me pretty, so give up!"

Aunt: "Stop frowning . . . you're going to get a line there . . ."

Other Aunt: "You better get married soon or you will grow a moustache!"

The women all laugh.

Aleko's voice: "Thomna!"

The women are immediately silent. Thomna goes to the door.

Thomna: "Yes, father."

Aleko's voice: "Our guest will try your coffee." Then to Stavros: "How do you like it?"

Stavros' voice: "Without sugar."

Aleko's voice: "You hear!?"

Thomna, turning back, whispers: "He has a very strong voice."

The women all giggle.

In the living room, Stavros is eating a Turkish Delight with all the condescension of an affluent young man born to means.

Stavros: "Very nice, very nice."

Aleko: "And this is my brother Seraphim."

Stavros, very traditional: "I kiss your mother's hand."

Aleko: "And this is my brother Protermos."

Some of the girls are peeking from out the kitchen door. They go back in the kitchen to compare opinions. A buzz is heard.

Stavros: "I kiss your mother's eyes."

Aleko: "And this—" He stops and suddenly calls off in the direction of the kitchen: "Anoola! Keep those women quiet in there. We can't hear each other with all that mzzzmzzz!"

Several anxious female faces look out the door, make gestures of servility and compliance, and so withdraw.

Aleko: "Women! God made the mistake of giving them tongues!"

All laugh as the tradition demands. Meantime the men are appraising Stavros and comparing notes.

The coffee is ready in the kitchen. It is poured into cups and put on a tray, which is then given to Thomna to bring in and serve to the men.

A Sister: "He is handsome, Thomna, I took a good look at him and he is handsome. Oh Thomna!"

Aunt: "Has he money?"

Thomna: "I don't know."

Anoola: "Your father will find that out."

Thomna carries the tray into the living room. She walks slowly up to Stavros and serves him. The game is that neither lets it be seen that they are inspecting the other. He is, after all, talking about more important things with the men. She is ever demure.

Stavros: "Oh, my father? My father is in various lines, different businesses."

Stavros and Thomna, deeply aware of each other, show nothing.

Aleko: "Fine, fine, a great variety of enterprises is wise."

Stavros takes a coffee from the tray Thomna extends to him. "One goes down, the other comes up!"

Thomna takes a swift look at Stavros. From the kitchen one hears the polite laughter of the women. Stavros takes a swift look at Thomna. As she hurries off, Thomna gives her father a lightning glance . . . assent! Meantime . . .

Uncles, a murmur of bees: "Exactly! Exactly! How wise! Yes . . . yes . . ."

The women are waiting anxiously. Thomna enters the kitchen with the biggest news of the decade!

Thomna: "He has a moustache!!!"

And she begins to cry. The strain.

Anoola: "Thomna dear, dear Thomna, many men have moustaches."

Thomna, crying: "I like it, I like it!"

In the living room the men talk.

Stavros, innocently: "That was Thomna?"

Uncles: "Yes . . . yes . . ."

All look to see what impression she made on Stavros.

Stavros seems pleased, even pleasantly surprised. "Oh!—oh! . . . Oh!!"

Aleko gives an almost imperceptible nod of approval to Our Cousin. The deal is on! Everybody knows it. A general murmur.

Aleko: "Perhaps on one of your father's business trips here we can have a coffee together and . . ."

Aleko is suddenly minimizing the matter of

money. Impulsively he throws his arm around the boy's shoulders.

Aleko: "At last I'm going to have a son!!"

General laughter.

Back home a letter full of good news has arrived.

Vasso: "Look! Look, her picture!"

All rush to see. A long look.

Isaac, the best he can do: "She must be a very good cook!"

Aunt: "They say that a long nose is a sign of virtue."

Old Uncle: "With a nose like that, virtue is inevitable."

Vasso: "They have money though. Listen to this." She reads: " 'They insisted I give up the work I was in and—' " She stops. Suspiciously, "Did he ever say *what* work he was in?? No!" She continues reading: " 'And so—what could I do? I accepted a position in their firm.' "

The Sinyosoglou Carpet Company is clearly a prosperous establishment. Like Our Cousin's, it is located in an arcade, a large one, a street roofed in glass. Soft, grimy daylight filters down to the various commercial enterprises. Standing in front of the store is Stavros, the model now of the prosperous young businessman, again wearing wing collar and frock coat.

In the back of the store the brothers and Our Cousin are in hot negotiation. Stavros cannot hear their words.

A beggar comes by, solicits a coin from Stavros. Stavros ignores him. As the beggar moves off, Stavros notices his shoes. They are the ones he gave to a beggar long ago on the road outside his village.

Stavros looks up. It is indeed Hohanness. He is on the verge of collapse, hungry, sick, exhausted. He leans against a store front for a moment. It is the window of the store next to the Sinyosoglou Carpet Company, and the porter in charge comes out and drives him off. Stavros catches up with Hohanness. Hohanness, thinking Stavros another enemy, cowers, covering his head. Stavros lifts Hohanness' head gently.

Stavros: "Don't you remember me?!!" He points to his feet. "Those are my shoes!!!"

Hohanness, hazily: "Oh! Yes . . . Yes, I remember."

And then some emotion he can't understand takes hold of Stavros. He embraces Hohanness passionately, wildly, as if the boy were in fact the only friend he had in the world.

Stavros whispers hoarsely: "You made it to here . . . Allah!" He comes closer. In a fanatical, conspiratorial tone: "See! We're going to get there!"

Hohanness: "I don't know. I used to think so, but . . ."

He has a fit of coughing, through which he smiles apologetically.

Stavros: "Don't give up! Don't give up now! You're just hungry. Are you hungry?"

Hohanness smiles, gently, warily: "I'm always hungry."

Stavros: "Come."

He takes Hohanness' hand and leads him off. Within minutes they are in a restaurant.

Stavros: "Eat, eat! I have money. Another?" He shouts imperiously. "Waiter! Bring another of these. Immediately. And more bread!" Then he leans forward, whispers: "Put some bread inside your shirt. Here! Here! And another piece. Go on, you'll need it later. No one's looking."

And now even more confidentially: "You have to look out for yourself in this world, you know. The only bad times I've had was when I was —well, soft! You can't afford to be. People take advantage. For instance, you! You smile all the time. People take it—forgive me for saying so— people take it as a sign of weakness. Now, suddenly, people respect me more. Even you do. Right? You respect me more. Don't you? Eh? Eh?"

In the back of the Sinyosoglou Brothers' store, the five brothers, Stavros, and Our Cousin are gathered.

Aleko: "So I have decided. My daughter shall come to you with five hundred Turkish pounds."

Stavros: "I do not accept."

There is a moment of bewilderment. The boy has spoken abruptly, absolutely, and even with some arrogance. Aleko, puzzled, tries hard to be patient, understanding.

Aleko: "Why, my son, why, what do you want?"

Stavros: "One hundred and ten pounds."

All burst out laughing. Except Our Cousin. But his protests are lost in the burst of amusement and surprise.

Aleko studies the boy. "There's something about you I don't understand." There is a little anxious moment of silence. "Have it your way. So—one hundred and ten it is. Satisfied?"

Stavros: "Yes, that is satisfactory."

Aleko: "Well, then, smile! Don't you ever smile?"

Stavros smiles. They all laugh. The meeting breaks up. Aleko goes to Stavros and walks off with him, arm around him. The others follow.

Aleko: "So when will it be? Two months?"

Stavros: "The sooner the better."

Aleko: "So, two months! Good! And one small thing—it is our understanding that you will live here with us. You will not take our daughter away from us."

Stavros answers without hesitation: "I will not take your daughter away."

It is several weeks later. In the Sinyosoglou apartment, Thomná can be seen coming through the door from the kitchen carrying a tray which holds six little cups of coffee. She goes to a coffee table and sets it down.

It is a Sunday afternoon, right after dinner. The five brothers and Stavros are sitting around the coffee table, stunned by the impact of the meal they've just devoured. The women, who by tradition eat much less, are in the kitchen doing the dishes and cleaning up.

Aleko releases a sort of sigh: "Ach . . . ach . . ."

Other Brothers: "Ach . . . ach . . . ach . . ."

Aleko: "Too much. Too much food!"

Other Brothers: "Too much! Too much!"

More sighs. Then, one by one, they undo the top buttons of their trousers, and thus ease out their bellies.

Aleko: "I tell those women don't put so much food on the table, but they don't listen."

Suddenly he seizes Thomna and takes her off into the farthest corner of the room to a large overstuffed armchair. Aleko falls into it and pulls his daughter down onto his lap. She puts her head on his shoulder. He embraces her lovingly.

Stavros' face is a mask.

Aleko: "So! One more week and I lose my daughter." Thomna buries her face in his shoulder. "Happy?"

Thomna:. "Baba, I'm frightened!"

Aleko: "Naturally. But you like him?"

Thomna: "Oh, yes, yes—but he's so mysterious!"

Aleko: "Maybe he's frightened too. What does he say when you're alone?"

Thomna: "Nothing."

Aleko: "Nothing?"

Thomna; "And we're never alone."

Aleko: "Well, I give you permission. Just be careful."

Thomna: "There's nothing to be careful about. He sits there and looks into space, says yes, says no, says nothing. It's as if he has a secret."

Aleko: "He's never talked to you?"

Thomna: "Never. Yes, once. He showed me some pictures in a book."

Aleko: "Pictures?"

Thomna: "A city in America. Very tall buildings. And he told me about them, how tall they were and all that as if he'd been there."

Aleko: "Oh well . . ."

Thomna: "He said he once had a dream to go there. I didn't know what to say."

Aleko: "Oh, all boys have dreams. I had the same dreams once. To go to a new land, start again. But people think one way when they're penniless and another way when the money comes."

Thomna: "Oh, Baba, Baba, I wish he were more like . . . like . . ."

She kisses him, tears in her eyes.

Aleko: "Well no one's as good as your Baba!" They enjoy a good laugh together. "We'll make him forget all that other. I'll give him money and you give him babies. And your mother flesh to put on his bones. And, so, he'll grow up and be a man!!"

Thomna: "Oh, Baba, yes, Baba, yes. Oh—I feel better!"

Aleko pulls her closer and whispers: "I have a little surprise for you both this afternoon. You'll see!" He looks towards Stavros. "Look! Look at him. See!"

Stavros is unbuttoning the top of his trousers. Then he catches Thomna and Aleko looking at him and quickly rebuttons. Aleko and Thomna laugh. She again embraces her father happily.

Aleko: "Go on, go on! It's no shame. Let the stomach out. It's natural!!"

Stavros is embarrassed, shakes his head.

One of the Brothers: "He's shy."

They all laugh, their bellies shaking. Anoola comes out of the kitchen to see what's up.

Aleko: "Anoola!! no supper tonight! I shall not eat again till tomorrow!"

Anoola: "You'll feel different in a few hours."

One of the Brothers: "Maybe in an hour." All the brothers laugh.

Aleko: "I don't want to see food again today! That's final!"

Katie, the youngest sister, is showing Stavros a book of photographs. She is about thirteen.

Aleko: "Katie, what are you showing him?"

Katie: "Pictures of the island."

Aleko: "Yes, the island. We have a beautiful place there, my boy. This summer we'll go there. We have two donkeys. We'll pack them and go for a picnic."

Anoola: "He's talking about more food already."

Aleko: "By next summer I will have digested this meal. Yes, there are some beautiful places there for a picnic." Anoola says something. "What? Oh. Anoola doesn't like flying insects." Anoola makes a sound of disgust. "So we'll have the picnic on our porch. It's screened. Any king would be lucky to have it. And you and I will sit there, Stavros. Plenty of women to look after us. And we'll wait! The years will pass." Anoola says something. "What? Oh. I know it takes only nine months. Whatever it takes, we'll wait. Nine months, ten, so long as it's a boy. A son. Then another. Two sons first. After that, I don't care." Anoola again. "What? I know you can't order what you want. Who should know better?" Then to Stavros: "But give me two sons and I'll give you my business. Everything! I mean, my share. My brothers are there, of course. But there is plenty for everybody. Just give me two sons. Then watch the years pass. The winters here. The summers on the Island. Before you know it, Stavros, your eldest will come to you and say, 'Father! I have found a girl. I want to be married.' And you will say, 'How much has she got? What dowry will she bring?'" All laugh. "And you'll get heavier and Thomna will get bigger, certain places especially, like Anoola." Anoola squawks. "All right, Anoola, I didn't say where. And watch the years pass! And you'll be old and I'll be old and we'll sit here together and drink and eat and undo the tops of our trousers and take a nap right here, side by side, a little nap and the women will 'mmzzmzzzmzzz' from the kitchen. Then we'll wake and play backgammon. And then all of a sudden it will be time for a little Ouzo and some olives and cheese and all my children and all your children will be here together." He sighs, "Ach, ach, aman!"

They all sigh: "Ach . . . ach . . . ach . . ."

Aleko: "And only you and I will talk, Stavros, because I taught my women *respect!* And when you talk everyone will keep quiet. And when I talk even you will keep quiet. And when we die, we will die properly! Surrounded by women looking after us! How does that sound to you?"

Stavros' eyes are half closed, but they are moist. The goodness and the warmth of this family has affected him deeply. Thomna is watching him anxiously.

Stavros, softly: "It's all a man should want."

The girls come in, finished with the cleaning up. Aleko suddenly rises.

Aleko: "Come on, now, get up, everybody get up. I've got something to show you. Come, come, Stavros, everybody!"

There is a general babble. The sisters are singing softly. Others join in. The group follows Aleko out of the apartment.

Aleko leading, the group comes out of the Sinyosoglou apartment, some singing, some humming or laughing. It is family life at its most seductive.

As they follow, Thomna does something which is, for her, very bold. She puts her arm around Stavros' waist. Aleko leads the way up the stairs.

Stavros: "Who lives up here?"

Thomna doesn't know. She is singing but

makes a sign to say it's all a pleasant mystery to her. At the landing above, Aleko takes a key out of his pocket and opens the door of an apartment. He throws the door open, then turns, full of his happy surprise.

Aleko: "Stavros! Here!" He turns and gives the boy a key. "Go on in, it's yours! Thomna! Go on!"

The gift apartment is entirely furnished and ready for immediate occupancy. In fact, it has the stuffy, overcomfortable look of an apartment that has been lived in for years by a home-loving couple with a habit of collecting things. Anoola and the girls have been working on it for weeks.

Everything that is happening makes it tougher for Stavros.

It is a complete surprise for Thomna also. Her eyes fill with tears, and she turns and rushes to embrace her father. At this there is a hubbub. Katie is crying, the uncles laughing and examining things. Anoola rushes to Stavros.

Anoola: "See this . . . this . . . it was my father's . . . when he died."

Stavros: "What?"

Aleko: "Everything here belonged to someone in the family who later died! I don't know what she's trying to say about it, but don't bother!"

Thomna: "Baba . . ."

She goes close to whisper.

Aleko: "Yes, my heart."

Thomna: "Oh Baba, thank you, but please, take everyone away now, please. I want to find out how *he* likes it."

From the door, Katie and Stavros are looking into the bedroom. Katie is making her first experiment with the opposite sex:

Katie: "Oh . . . this is the bedroom . . ."

Stavros: "Yes."

Katie blushes. From a distance, she hears her father's voice. At the door of the apartment Aleko is gathering his family and ushering them out.

Aleko: "Katie! Come on now, stop bothering Stavros." Then he turns on the others: "Go on, go on, go on."

As she goes, Katie whispers to Aleko.

Katie: "He likes me."

She exits. Aleko throws an apprehensive look back at Thomna, then exits too. The door closes. Thomna crosses to the door and locks it. Then she goes to the bedroom.

Stavros is at the window of the bedroom. The sun is coming through. Thomna moves softly to her husband-to-be and looks at him. It is the first time they've been alone, the first time she has looked at him as directly as she has wanted to, her first chance to get close to him. Stavros has been very affected by the warmth and the generosity of the Sinyosoglous.

Thomna, softly: "Stavros."

Stavros: "You have a fine family. Your father is a king. A king."

Thomna: "But sometimes I think we are too many girls. May God forgive me, I have often wished my sisters were brothers."

She laughs nervously.

Stavros: "I like your family."

Thomna, daring: "Do you like me?"

Stavros: "Yes."

Thomna: "Would you tell me if you didn't?"

The question is so simple and direct, yet so probing, Stavros can't but tell the truth.

Stavros: "No . . . I wouldn't."

Thomna, after a pause: "Well . . ."

Stavros: "But I do like you."

Thomna, daring again: "In the way a husband should like a wife?"

Stavros: "Well . . ."

Thomna: "I'm sorry. You don't have to say anything to that."

An awkward pause.

Stavros: "Shall we go?"

Thomna, quickly: "No, let's stay here. I've never talked to you without my family."

Stavros: "Oh, yes. We have."

Thomna: "If you say so. When?"

Stavros: "Several times."

Thomna: "Yes, of course.

A silence.

Thomna: "Stavros!"

Stavros: "Yes, Thomna?"

Thomna: "Is there anything you want to say to me?"

Stavros: "No."

Thomna: "Please don't take offense at what I'm about to say. I've often felt that you have some worry, some secret that you're not . . ."

Stavros: "No, no."

Thomna: "Not that I'll expect you to tell me everything. Or anything, if you don't want to. I want everything to be the way you want it to be. Do you hear?"

Stavros: "Yes, Thomna."

Thomna: "I wish I were prettier for you."

Stavros: "Don't worry about that."

Thomna: "But I'm a good girl. You'll see. I'm a good girl. You just tell me what you want me to do. I'll do whatever you tell me."

Stavros: "Yes, Thomna. Don't cry, Thomna, don't."

Suddenly a crack in the wall around his tension.

Stavros, sharply: "Don't cry. Thomna, stop crying!"

Thomna: "Stop . . . Yes . . . Yes . . . I have."

Stavros: "What's the matter?"

Thomna: "I'm frightened."

Stavros: "Of what?"

Thomna: "Of your silence. Say something!"

Then she practically screams.

Thomna: "Say something! Say something! Say something, something, something!"

She recovers. Or seems to.

Thomna: "I'm sorry. I've felt nervous all morning. I had a dream last night. May I tell you?"

Stavros: "If you like."

Thomna, almost hysterical again: "Do you want to hear it or don't you? Do you want to hear it?"

Stavros: "Would you like a glass of water?"

Thomna: "No." She recovers somewhat. "Oh, I'm ashamed of myself. I'm ashamed . . . silly, silly . . . I'm acting like a . . . young girl. And I'm three years older than you. They didn't tell you that."

Stavros: "It doesn't make any difference."

Thomna: "I dreamt that we had a child. He looked like you, fuzzy brown hair all over his head, and so soft everywhere, and the back of his neck straight and proud like yours. And the little thing was hungry. So I opened myself to feed it, and it came with its mouth to me—and there was no milk. I had no milk. It pulled at me and pulled at me . . ."

Stavros: "Don't worry, you will have."

Thomna: "I don't know if I can tell you the rest."

Stavros, touched by her now: "Of course, go on."

Thomna, laughing nervously: "Turn your head away a little. . . . It had teeth. And the teeth hurt. The baby child turned into you. I mean—it was you. And you pulled back and looked at me with such disappointment. And then you walked away and I never saw you again."

Stavros: "Oh."

Thomna: "Do you believe in dreams?"

Stavros: "Yes."

Thomna: "Are you going to do that?"

Stavros: "Yes."

Stavros absolutely didn't expect to say this. The question was put to him quickly and suddenly, and his answer popped out spontaneously. At that instant, he was full of feeling for Thomna.

She is speechless. Then . . .

Thomna: "Stavros? Stavros? What did you say? Stavros?"

It's a question she's frightened to ask, but must.

Only now does he realize what he has revealed. He is stunned by the sudden confrontation of what he is and what he has done.

Thomna: "Stavros . . ."

Stavros: "This—I did this—because—" He can't go on. "Count yourself lucky. You won't see me again."

Thomna: "Stavros . . ."

Stavros: "One hundred and ten Turkish pounds is the fare to the United States of America."

Thomna: "America? America?"

Stavros: "By the first boat."

Thomna: "I don't understand." Then she begins to. "Oh . . . America?"

Stavros: "Yes."

Thomna: "And you—?"

Stavros: "Yes."

Thomna: "Oh." She can't speak for a moment. Then, "I still don't understand. You wanted it so much that . . . ?"

Stavros: "You have to be a person like I am to understand."

Thomna: "What will you do now?"

Stavros: "I don't know. I don't care. Something."

She goes towards him.

Thomna, gently: "If you want to take our

money and . . . go . . . to the United States of America . . ."

Stavros: "No."

Thomna: "I'm yours. What I have is yours."

He can hardly believe his ears.

Stavros: "How can you be like that?"

Thomna: "I have no reason to live except you." She looks at him lovingly—nakedly. "I wish I were prettier for you."

Stavros: "How can anybody be like that?"

At last he thinks of her.

Stavros: "Thomna, don't trust me. For your happiness, don't trust me."

Thomna: "You're all I have."

Stavros bows his head: "Don't trust me!"

Now Thomna, for the first time, goes to him spontaneously.

Thomna: "But Stavros, my soul, it will pass. Baba said so! It will pass like a sickness. When we once have children you won't feel the same, you can't, how could you??" She notices some reaction, goes on: "What? What?" There is no answer, "Stavros, it will pass, I know. I'll count on it."

Stavros: "Don't count on it."

A pause. There is something terrifying about the boy's silence. Abruptly, now, he gets up and starts for the door. Thomna cries out: "Where are you going?"

He stops and waits, but without making connection.

Thomna: "A year. Wait a year. Then if you . . ."

Pause. No answer. He is completely back in his shell.

Thomna: "Well, it's for you to decide. I'll not say anything to my father. I'll wait."

He exits. She sits there, alone, in their apartment.

5

The next day, in the Sinyosoglou Carpet Company, an event is taking place. Mr. Aratoon Kebabian, one of the big buyers from America, has come to Constantinople to make his season's buy. A business like that of the Sinyosoglou Brothers is built upon the favor of a handful of big buyers, mostly from America. Everything is done to win their favor.

Stavros and some porters are carrying a folded Sarouk carpet. Stavros is tense and silent. A porter scolds him.

Aleko: "Come, come, come, hurry, hurry." He turns to Mr. Aratoon Kebabian, selling hard: "I saved these thirty pieces of Sarouk nine by twelve just for *you!* Ask the boys! Boys!?"

Porters mutter: "Yes, sir."

Aleko: "In the back of the store! Like eggs under a hen!"

He grabs a corner of the rug that Stavros and the porters are unfolding and drags it over to Aratoon Kebabian, where he is seated, a king in a straw hat. At his side has been placed a small table which holds sweets and a nargileh, a water pipe, from which he takes an occasional puff. He is a man of seventy-two but looks a little younger —except in the morning when he looks considerably older. He carries amber beads which keep running through his fingers. He dresses as if he were going to his seat in the enclosure at Belmont Race Track.

Aleko: "You know rugs better than I. You know you've never seen anything like these pieces! Here! Butter! Feel, feel!"

Suddenly Aleko changes his course. Taking the Sarouk by the corner he drags it with the aid of Stavros and the porters to Mrs. Kebabian.

Aleko: "Mrs. Kebabian, I beg you, put your hand on this Sarouk."

Aratoon: "She doesn't know anything about the rug business except how to live off it."

Aleko: "Only for her pleasure. Feel it!" He turns, sharply, to Stavros. "Stavros, will you for God's sake wake up and bring the rug here! What's the matter with you today?"

Sophia: "Please don't inconvenience yourself. I don't like rugs."

Since she is not interested in rugs, Aleko brings her Stavros.

Aleko: "Mrs. Kebabian, may I present the future king. One day all this will be his. Stavros Topouzoglou, my future son-in-law. Come Stavros, kiss Mrs. Kebabian's hand."

Sophia Kebabian is a woman of forty-four, dark, slender, elegant, worldly, remote. She has the high coloring of the secret drinker. She notices that Stavros is all charged up.

Sophia: "You don't have to kiss my hand, boy."

Aleko: "Oh, of course, of course, in America they don't do that. Show him how they do in America, Mrs. Kebabian. Believe me when I tell you that this boy's *dream* is America!"

Sophia: "Mr. Sinyosoglou, don't sell me, sell my husband."

Stavros likes her. Her mood fits his. Aleko laughs uncomfortably. He is not used to women "talking back."

Sophia continues to Aleko: "He is going to buy. He's only first torturing you a little."

A tray of drinks is passed. Aratoon anxiously watches his wife to see if she takes one.

Sophia: "Oh, no, no, no, thank you."

Aleko: "Show him how they do in America. Go on!"

Sophia: "Well . . ."

She extends her hand. Stavros takes it tentatively.

Sophia: "No, not that way. Take hold of it.

Good! Now shake it. Like this!"

Stavros: "You do this? In America? I mean men to women?"

Sophia: "Of course."

Aleko, glad she likes the boy: "His whole dream—to go to America. Imagine!"

Sophia: "Well—people have done it."

Aleko: "But not a boy like this. Men!"

Stavros almost turns on him. Sophia marks this. Then Aleko notices something behind him, turns and runs to Aratoon, who is preparing to leave.

Aleko: "Aratoon! Where are you going?"

Aratoon: "Time to eat. My stomach is my clock."

Stavros, quietly to Sophia: "You are American?"

He has never seen an independent, sophisticated woman before. He studies her, fascinated with her manner, her stance, her clothes, her perfume. She *is* America to him.

Sophia: "Yes. I was born here, but Mr. Kebabian brought me to America twenty-five years ago when we married and I . . ."

She raises her veil. She looks at him. He looks at her.

Aratoon: "Sophia, are you coming?"

Sophia: "No, I'm not."

Aleko: "Oh, you must. They're waiting for us

at Abdullah's. I spoke to the chef myself. You should have seen his face when I said Mr. and Mrs. Aratoon Kebabian." He turns to Aratoon. "Everything you ever ate and remarked on there is ready. She must come!" Then to Mrs. Kebabian: "You got thinner."

Aratoon: "She doesn't eat. I married a *woman. Now* look!"

Sophia: "I don't enjoy eating when I'm not hungry."

Stavros smiles at her— a fellow rebel.

Aratoon: "You see how she talks back! They ruined her. The day she became an American citizen—ruined!" To his wife: "The Declaration of Independence was politics! Only! Not for women!!" Then to Aleko: "Come. No hope for her!" To his wife: "I'm leaving the carriage."

He starts out.

Sophia has been shopping and has many packages.

Stavros: "May I help you carry them to your hotel?"

Sophia: "Why, yes, yes, why thank you."

Sophia and Stavros enter the Kebabian suite in the Pera Palace Hotel. She is exhilarated by the prospect of some kind of adventure, playing the part of a gay, sophisticated woman of the world. They are met by a German maid.

Sophia: "Bertha, get Mr. . . . ?"

Stavros: "Topouzoglou."

Sophia: "Some lunch."

Stavros: "No, don't trouble."

Sophia: "Bertha!"

Stavros: "No, too much trouble."

Sophia: "No trouble."

Stavros: "I don't enjoy eating when I'm not hungry."

Sophia: "Well, all Greeks are taught to refuse twice. I won't believe you till you've refused three times. What can I get you? You were so kind."

Stavros: "Nothing. Well . . . Nothing."

But he makes no move to go. A hesitation. He smiles nervously. Bertha is fussing with a wardrobe trunk in the background.

Stavros: "That is a whole bureau? A whole bureau! And it travels with you? May I . . . ?"

Sophia: "Yes. Bertha, show him."

Stavros goes to examine the wardrobe trunk.

Stovros: "America, America!"

Sophia smiles. The boy kneels before it.

Sophia: "And down there, you see, for shoes."

Stavros: "Do you have any magazines from there? Pictures? Newspapers?"

Sophia: "Yes. Would you like to look at them?"

Stavros smiles, nods.

Stavros: "Can I?"

It is much later. Sophia is in the bedroom, lying down, drinking. Bertha comes in.

Sophia, in a whisper: "Bertha."

Bertha: "Yes, Mrs. Kebabian."

Sophia: "Is he still here?"

Bertha: "Yes, Mrs. Kebabian."

Sophia gets up and crosses to the door between the bedroom and the parlor. She opens it very cautiously. Stavros is sitting on the floor still going over the magazines. Now he sees one of Aratoon's straw hats. He goes on tiptoe, puts it on. He looks at himself in a mirror and winks.

The boy affects Sophia. How? She doesn't know yet. But he awakens something in her long given up for dead. She drinks, then crosses to the mirror of her dressing table, sits, and looks at herself. If a look could speak, we would hear, "I am still a very handsome woman for my age." She drinks.

Stavros is back on the floor, looking at magazines, when behind him the door of the suite opens and in comes Aratoon Kebabian.

Aratoon, as he crosses into the bedroom: "You still here?"

The boy doesn't know what to say. But Aratoon has not waited for an answer, is already in the bedroom.

For some reason Stavros feels guilty. And a little frightened. He listens apprehensively.

Aratoon: "He's still here."

Sophia, lightly: "Oh yes, he's having dinner with us. He's going to show us some dancing."

Stavros looks up. Sophia comes to the door of the bedroom.

Sophia: "You know some place where we can see some dancing? You do, don't you?"

Stavros: "But of course."

He smiles. Now he knows she likes him.

$$\text{ʊʊʊ}$$

Later, in a night club, some of the male patrons are taking turns dancing in front of the line of musicians. At a ringside table, Sophia is drinking. Aratoon is eating as if he hadn't had lunch. The music comes to a pause.

Sophia, to Stavros: "I'd like to see you dance."

Stavros smiles. Then without a word, he walks towards the dance floor. He throws some money onto the musicians' platform. As they play, he begins to dance alone.

Sophia watches him. Aratoon finishes his food, looks at his hands which are covered with olive oil and meat fat, and decides to go to the washroom.

Stavros dances up to the table where Sophia is now alone. As he dances before her, in little rhythmic breaks, he makes slight hissing sounds, directed at her, seductive, insistent. Her cheeks burn. She covers them with her hands. Tears come to her eyes. She drinks.

Later, a lone musician improvises on the bouzouki. Aratoon has fallen fast asleep at the table. Stavros and Sophia, seated on either side of Aratoon, talk across him. Sophia is drunk now, but gently, soulfully. There is an element of bitter humor in what she says.

Sophia: "I was eighteen when my father said, 'Marry him!'" She indicates the sleeping Aratoon. "I'd never been permitted to see that wonder, a man, alone. Not till him." Again she nods a little sardonically at her sleeping husband. "The day after the wedding—*tack!* He took me to America. And before I knew how, I had two sons. And after that—what? He had what he wanted. And there I was—an old woman or so with two sons and a husband with a good business, who played cards every night. I've never known a young man. I never lived my twentieth year. Or my twenty-first. And my twenty-second year is still inside me, waiting like a live baby to be born, waiting inside me, you know? How could you know?"

She can't go on for weeping. Stavros looks at her with compassion. She looks at him—a longing, dependent look. He leans across the table, takes her hand, turns it open. Then he buries his mouth in the palm. He gets up, starts moving away, then puts his hand on her shoulder close to her neck.

Sophia is on fire for the first time in her life. Her eyes close. Her whole body trembles in a deep convulsion. She tries to pull her hand free, can't. Then she gives in to the paroxysm for a moment. Now she's out on the other side, weak, remote. She gently pulls her hand free.

Sophia now looks at Stavros—resentfully? She's never been in anyone's power before. And never expected to be. She turns to Aratoon. Some of the long strands of hair which he uses to cover his bald top have slipped. She replaces them gently. The bouzouki! She looks at Aratoon with a gentleness and a kindliness she's never felt before. She's free of him. She smiles, then turns to Stavros—now with him, therefore direct, even brusque.

Sophia: "Let's take him home."

In the office of the North German Lloyd Line, a ticket is being stamped with a quick forceful stroke of a mechanical validator. The official at the desk hands the ticket to a clerk, who gives him some money. Then the clerk takes the ticket and, crossing to the counter, hands it to Stavros.

In his hand at last, a ticket to America! Suddenly some pellets of paper hit him on the head. He hears laughter behind him.

Crouched against the wall behind him are eight boys, all in a row, all sitting upon their haunches, all about the same age and in the same condition of poverty and hope. They're grinning like little apes.

Stavros' anger these days is close to the surface. He spins around. Then he sees that one of the boys is Hohanness, who gives a little wave. Stavros goes to him.

Stavros: "You! You're going!?—Eh?" Hohanness nods. "Didn't I tell you, don't give up?? Tell me, come tell me what happened?"

Hohanness: "That man—he's taking us all."

A portly man, Mr. Demos Agnostis, is at the ticket counter buying steerage passage for the eight boys.

Stavros is unexpectedly agitated: "You're all going?"

Hohanness: "He has a place to shine shoes in New York City, and—"

Hohanness has a fit of coughing, can't continue.

One of the Boys: "He pays our passage. *The Kaiser Wilhelm.*"

Stavros: "And what? What do you—?"

The Boy: "We work for him. Two years without pay."

Stavros: "Oh?"

Some painful struggle can be seen on Stavros' face. Envy? Regret? Why did his heart sink?

Stavros: "Tell me . . . would he take another?"

Hohanness: "No, he'll only take eight. I came by the store once to tell you about it. I saw you get into a carriage with some rich men." He makes a graphic gesture in the neighborhood of his abdomen. "Plenty to eat! Plenty to eat! So I thought . . ."

Suddenly Stavros' mask of self-sufficiency is up again.

Stavros: "Well, of course! Two years without pay! That is slavery! What do you think I am? Allah!"

Hohanness: "For me, it's all right. Well, anyway, I see you're going."

Stavros: "Yes, don't worry about me. The same boat too! On the same boat!"

Hohanness: "How did you get the money? Well, of course—you have rich friends!"

Stavros, tough: "Yes. I have rich friends."

꩜

The room where Stavros lives is extremely bare. Some burlap thrown in a corner serves as a bed. There is no other furniture. He is crouching on the floor against the wall. He doesn't move from this defensive position. In front of him are two objects: A bundle of clothes, wrapped and tied in a throw rug, and, alongside, his hamal's harness.

Thomna: "But your soul, your everlasting soul!"

Stavros: "Rot my soul!"

Thomna: "Stavros, it's wrong. It's a sin!"

Stavros: "That right and wrong business is for the rich. You can afford it. I can't."

Thomna: "Stavros, you come from a good family!"

Stavros: "Yes! All now waiting for one piece of good news, at last—one piece of good news."

Thomna: "But your father? What will—"

Stavros: "I don't want to be my father. I don't want to be your father. I don't want that good family life. That good family life!" He is raving. "All those good people, they stay here and live in this shame! The churchgoers who give to the poor, live in this shame. The respectable ones, the polite ones, the good manners! But *I am going!* No matter how! No matter, no matter, no matter how!!"

He stops finally, recovers, speaks gently, firmly.

Stavros: "I wrote you to come here, because I wanted to speak to you the truth before I left. The truth of what I am, so you don't go on thinking about me."

She doesn't answer, looks at the objects on the floor.

Thomna: "What's this?" She indicates his hamal's harness. "Oh. You're taking this with you?"

Stavros: "Of course. You can't count on anybody or anything. With this, in America, I can always make to eat."

He fusses with the harness affectionately.

Thomna speaks gently now. She has given up: "Christ arisen protect you!"

Stavros: "I know that I'll never again find any-one like you."

Thomna, weeping: "Stavros, my heart, my soul, my very own soul, what will happen to you?"

And now for the first time in months and months Stavros softens; he too speaks gently, wist-fully.

Stavros: "I believe . . . I believe that . . . that in America . . . I believe I will be washed clean."

6

The prow of *The Kaiser Wilhelm* heads into a heavy sea. A massive wave breaks over the bow and flings itself on the foredeck.

Steerage. At the very point of the prow, looking ahead for land that will not appear for days, stand Stavros and Hohanness.

Bertha emerges from a companionway, followed by a sailor. They have traveled this route before. The sailor spots Stavros and approaches him. The ship is tossing. The steerage passengers huddle behind the deck machinery in little wet clusters.

The sailor has the working man's scorn for anything less than "honest" manual labor. He walks up to Stavros and stands in front of him, grinning.

Sailor: "Madam wants her bonbon."

Stavros, by now an expert at masking his true feelings, gives no recognition to this challenge. But the boy is beginning to feel the humiliation of his position. Hohanness doesn't understand quite what's happening, but he does see his friend's intense humiliation.

Stavros: "What are you looking at me that way for?"

Hohanness, softly: "Do you have to go?"

Stavros, tough: "I *want* to go." Then relenting, "I'll bring you some candy again."

Stavros feels criticized by the whole world. He assumes a defiant nonchalance as he starts off in the direction of Bertha. It's the only way he has found to live through his present circumstance.

The procession—Bertha, Stavros, and the sailor—arrives at the doors to the Kebabian suite. Bertha knocks softly on the first door. An answering signal. She turns to Stavros, speaks practically.

Bertha: "Madam prefers when you smile."

She opens the door deftly, admits Stavros, then proceeds to the next door, Aratoon Kebabian's bedroom, and enters. She closes the door swiftly and tiptoes to the bed. Aratoon is snoring heavily but quietly, an old man. Bertha sits in a chair by his bed, picks up some needlework, and begins to embroider.

The next day the sea is calm. The prow parts the waters. At the bow Hohanness is looking at Stavros. The "tougher" Stavros gets, the more understanding Hohanness becomes. He feels the other boy's shame through his mask, loves him for it.

Stavros, defiantly: "Stop looking at me that soft way all the time."

Hohanness turns away, embarrassed. Then he begins to cough. Each time he can't control his cough he looks around anxiously at Mr. Agnostis, nearby on the deck.

Stavros: "How long have you had it?"

Hohanness: "My cough? It's the first thing I remember."

He leans forward and whispers, touching his chest, smiling gently.

Hohanness: "I know what I have."

Stavros: "Quiet yourself." He tries to divert him. "They say tomorrow we see land."

Hohanness: "But before it eats me, if I can . . . Did I tell you?"

Stavros: "Another time . . . shshshsh . . ."

Hohanness: "At home every morning I go for water. And it's a walk. You know water is heavy! Well, now—I'm the only child—my mother goes.

So every morning I think of her making that walk. So before this eats me," he touches his chest, "I pray . . . to earn enough to put a well down for her."

He is getting excited and begins to cough, looking around to see if Mr. Agnostis is within earshot. A sharp whistle is heard.

Through the companionway comes the sailor for Stavros. Stavros goes a few steps toward the waiting sailor, then suddenly turns and comes back to Hohanness, speaks, for once, free of his mask of defiance.

Stavros: "At home I have three sisters and four brothers."

Hohanness doesn't get the point: "Oh . . . oh . . . ? Then . . ."

Stavros: "One by one, I'm going to bring them over. You'll see. You'll see."

Hohanness: "Well, naturally . . . that's the important thing. That's the only important thing . . . naturally."

Stavros in his most cocky manner now turns and goes toward the sailor.

By now Hohanness loves Stavros.

Hohanness speaks to himself: "What's more important? Naturally!"

Screaming sea gulls fly around the mast of *The Kaiser Wilhelm*. In the distance, coming out of a mist, the shore of Long Island. Hohanness, at the prow, turns, calls.

Hohanness: "Stavros! Stavros!!"

But Stavros is not there.

The steerage passengers come to take their first look. Heads appear in the portholes. These people are very poor and from every country served by the Mediterranean. They are still in their native clothes, their possessions bundled and always at their sides. Italians. Romanians. Albanians. Russians. Serbs. Croats. Syrians. Bearded Orthodox Jews. Fanatics. Men alone. An occasional child with a tag around his neck.

In his cabin, Aratoon Kebabian awakes. Bertha is at his side, working on her embroidery.

Aratoon: "What's the disturbance?"

Bertha: "Long Island."

Aratoon, dismissing it: "Oh, well. How long did I sleep?"

Bertha: "A couple of hours."

They hear a low commotion from Sophia's room. Stavros, despite objection from Sophia, is preparing to rush up on deck.

Bertha, quickly: "I'll tell Mrs. Kebabian you're awake."

She goes to the door between the two state-rooms and enters Sophia's room as deftly as she can. Aratoon listens.

Bertha: "Mr. Kebabian is awake."

Whispering, footsteps, the door to the outer corridor opening, and closing. Aratoon enjoys an immense yawn. Bertha re-enters.

Bertha: "She'll be in as soon as she's pretty."

Aratoon: "I have a long wait." Now he fixes Bertha with his eye. "Bertha! Bertha! Now come, Bertha!"

Bertha, facing him: "Mr. Kebabian I try hard. I try hard to be for her and to be for you. You know how she is. You know—how she is."

Aratoon: "I also know who pays your salary. Do you?"

Bertha: "Yes sir."

Aratoon: "Well then, let me hear. Order me some tea, some English tea, and then let me hear."

On the front deck, Stavros runs up to Hohanness. The other boys and Mr. Agnostis are also there.

Hohanness: "Stavros! Look, look! Mr. Agnostis says that is the city of Coney Island."

Stavros: "Those curves! What are they?"

Hohanness, authoritatively; "The Americans build roads through the air."

Stavros and Hohanness look at the promised land. Then Hohanness begins to cough painfully. He is instantly apprehensive that Mr. Agnostis will notice. He throws his whole face into the hollow of Stavros' shoulder and smothers the cough. Stavros is slightly embarrassed at the embrace. He makes a face. He tries to quiet Hohanness by diverting him as one would a child.

Stavros: "Here. Here, Hohanness, stop it. Look, here. I brought you some candy again. Here."

Hohanness, with difficulty: "One thing . . . that lady . . . friend of yours . . . has the most wonderful candy!"

He takes a piece.

Elsewhere on the deck, a number of the older passengers, including family groups, some women holding babies, are singing a Ukrainian song, full of longing.

Hohanness has recovered. He and Stavros drink in the shore line.

Night falls, and Hohanness and Stavros are just where they were. But the deck behind them is almost deserted. The two boys are singing a song for each other. It comes to its end.

Hohanness: "We'll always be friends."

Stavros: "Life's not like that. It's all meetings and partings."

Hohanness: "My father liked this one. Every Sunday, 'Hohanness! Come! Sing!'"

He starts to sing the song which Vartan and Stavros sang at the beginning of this story, on the mountain side. Stavros joins in, and as he sings, he takes off Vartan's fez, which he's worn all through, looks at it, and then drops it into the water of the bay.

Stavros: "First thing tomorrow, I'll get one of those straw hats the Americans wear. Tomorrow!"

Aratoon has wrung the story from Bertha, and the time has come. In his bedroom, still in bed, he is cutting Stavros down.

Aratoon: "So tomorrow, since you are without protector or guaranteed employment, the authorities will ship you back, back where you came from. And now may I gave you some advice? Go fall on your knees before Aleko Sinyosoglou. Shed a tear or two, however false, kiss his hand, and so on. He'll take you back. His daughter is so ugly he has no choice. Well?" Stavros is silent. "And from this unpleasantness, learn a lesson—when you force a woman to choose, she will choose money. Well?"

Stavros: "She's a good person."

Aratoon: "She's in the next room now, her ear to the door, hearing every word. Why is she silent? Well?" Stavros is silent. "What are you going to do now? Eh? You know I've never seen a face like yours except in a cage. I have a feeling there's nothing you'd stop at. Is there? Anything? Have you any honor?"

Stavros: "My honor is safe inside me."

A sadism emerges in the old man.

Aratoon: "What? What? Safe inside you?? Boy, whatever you ever once were, you are now a whore! A boy whore! For sale! You understand? Stop that humming! I've seen hundreds like you. Boys who leave home to find a clean life and just get dirtier and dirtier. Will you stop that humming! And tell me: Have you looked in the mirror recently? Truthfully, do you suppose if your father saw you at this moment he'd recognize his son? Would he know who you are?"

Choked cries of pain escape the boy's tight mouth, but so wretched, they afford no relief.

The door of the bedroom is flung open and Sophia rushes in. Bertha stands in the doorway.

Sophia: "Stop it! Stop it!"

Aratoon: "Go back in your room immediately."

In the corridor outside, two stewards and a sailor have been placed on guard.

Sophia: "Stop doing that to him. Stop doing that! He did more for me in two weeks than you did in your whole life!"

Stavros leads Sophia back to the door.

Stavros: "Sophia, go on. Go on now."

Sophia: "He's not going to do that to you."

Stavros: "It's all right. I'm this far. Thank you for bringing me this far."

He closes the door and faces Aratoon. In a way he is relieved that it's over, even though once again he has to find a new way for himself.

Stavros: "Mr. Kebabian."

Aratoon: "Ah! He's going to speak."

Stavros: "Yes sir." There is a pause. "I have nothing to say."

Aratoon: "What can you say? The truth is the truth. You know what you are."

Stavros: "Yes sir. Except . . . Mr. Kebabian, I've been beaten, robbed, shot, left for dead. I've eaten what was thrown to the dogs and driven the dogs off to get at it. I became a hamal and—"

Aratoon: "NOOOOWWW! Now you understand yourself—a hamal!"

Stavros: "Yes sir. But now, I'm here. I've seen the shore and their city in the distance. Do you imagine anyone will be able to keep me out?"

Aratoon: "I'll see to it."

Stavros: "I'll find a way, I'll find a—" He stops, realizes what the old man has said. "What did you say? What?"

Aratoon reaches for the bell to summon the steward.

Aratoon: "I said I'll see to it. *I'll see to it that they send you back.*"

Stavros leaps on top of the old man, one hand covering his mouth, the other at his throat before he can ring the bell. Bertha enters from the other room.

Stavros: "Swear! Swear you won't say or do anything, anything!"

Bertha has crossed to the corridor door and flung it open.

Bertha: "Help! Help! Help!"

The stewards and the sailor rush in. Stavros is pulled off Aratoon. Blows, curses, commotion. And all through, Bertha screaming: "Swine! Swine!"

Aratoon: "He attacked me! He tried to kill me! Intent to kill, intent to kill! He's a criminal!"

The two stewards and the sailor drag Stavros through the cabin door. Aratoon follows.

Aratoon: "This is America, hamal! Do you hear? This is America! What will you do now, hamal? What will you do now? Eh, eh, hamal?"

In a sudden last desperate explosion, the boy turns on his tormentors, punching, scratching, biting, kicking. And this time they beat him into final submission and drag him off, limp and silent.

⚓︎

The ship's doctor is a small, worn German, wearing a soiled white jacket. He is soaking a cloth in antiseptic. Now he carries it to where Stavros is lying on a cot in the Ship's Hospital, third class. Hohanness is there. Stavros winces as the doctor applies the cloth.

The Doctor: "A man shouldn't be hit on the head. It's not as hard as it feels. Let him sleep."

Hohanness: "I'll stay with him."

In the middle of the night, Stavros has his first nightmare. Hohanness is on the floor beside him.

Stavros, whispering: "Hohanness!! Hohanness!!"

Hohanness: "Yes, yes, I'm here."

Stavros: "Is my father still here?"

Hohanness: "Your what? What? Oh, no, no."

Stavros: "Isn't that—? Who's that?"

Hohanness: "The doctor."

Stavros: "Is he listening? Can he hear us?"

Hohanness: "He's asleep. Don't worry."

Stavros, conspiratorial: "My father said: 'That's enough. I'm ashamed of you. I'm ashamed of what you've made of yourself. Come back, you must start again!'" He bursts out laughing. "It hurts when I laugh. But can you imagine? Making this journey all over again? Allah!!"

Hohanness: "Shshsh. That was a dream. Go to sleep."

Stavros: "Allah! Hohanness, can you imagine?" Again he laughs, again it hurts. "Hohanness, stay with me."

Hohanness: "I'll be here when you wake."

Stavros is almost asleep now. His face darkens, he looks troubled.

Stavros: "You know the truth? The thing I'd like most in the world is to start this journey over. That's the truth! Just to start it over, all over again . . . oh . . . oh . . ."

Hohanness is very moved. Suddenly he has a

terrible fit of coughing. His eyes swing around to the doctor, who is awakened by Hohanness' cough.

Doctor: "How is he?"

Hohanness, frightened: "He's imagining things."

Doctor: "Well, no wonder! He was hit on the head once too often. You better watch over him. Stay close to him."

Hohanness: "I will."

Doctor: "He's liable to do something crazy. Goodnight. That's a bad cough you've got yourself. Better not let the Americans hear that tomorrow. They'll send you back."

On the front deck the next day, one sees very little for the fog. *The Kaiser Wilhelm* is moving slowly forward. The usual harbor noises. Out of the fog, as if coming toward the ship, is the Statue of Liberty. As they see it, the passengers stand. There is a sound—is it imagined?—of a general sigh.

A large motor launch is coming alongside.

Officials of the United States Health Service prepare to board ship.

Stavros wears a bandage. There is about him the manic desperation of the suicide-to-be.

One of the shoeshine boys has been sent to fetch Hohanness. He calls him, waves, calls again . . .

Hohanness starts off. Stavros pulls him back and, in whispers, gives him his final instructions.

Stavros: "It's the excitement that brings on your cough. So, close your ears. Imagine you've just put down your well. And your mother and father come to you in gratitude. Can you imagine that scene?"

Hohanness: "Oh, yes, yes!"

Stavros: "I'll wait for you just down the corridor. The instant the inspection is over, run to me."

He indicates to Hohanness he can go, pushes him off, but the boy comes back.

Hohanness: "But you, what are you going to do?"

Stavros: "I have my own plans."

Hohanness comes close, whispers.

Hohanness: "What?"

Stavros makes a subtle proud little gesture which says, "Over the side and swim for it."

Hohanness: "Can you swim that far?"

Stavros turns his face away: "They say a man learns what is necessary to save his life."

Hohanness: "Stavros, if you can't swim, you can't swim."

Stavros: "You better go. Go on, go on."

Hohanness: "And if you go down?"

Stavros: "Better than going back." He pushes him off. "Go on! They're waiting."

Hohanness seizes Stavros' hand and kisses it.

Hohanness: "I'll pay you back, some day. I'll pay you back . . ."

Stavros, tough: "Let's speak the truth. We'll never see each other after tomorrow. You'll forget me. And I? I'll be where I am."

᠕᠕᠕

The shoeshine boys are all gathered in their little cabin, sitting on the edge of their bunks. Mr. Agnostis and the Public Health official are in the middle of the floor.

Mr. Agnostis: "Same as last year. Eight fine boys."

Hohanness is following Stavros' instructions. One side of his head is pressed hard into the pillow. A hand covers the other ear. He is imagin-

ing the scene at the well and his parents' gratitude.

Mr. Agnostis: "All from fine families. Perfect
health. Employment guaranteed. Nothing to
worry. Everything under control!"

At the end of the corridor, Stavros waits.

Hohanness' eyes shine with his imaginings.
Health Official: "OK, OK."

He comes out of the shoeshine boys' cabin
and heads in the direction of Stavros, behind him
the first buzz of celebration.

Stavros waits for the official to pass him. Behind him sounds of the boys celebrating are
heard. Then suddenly we hear, dominating all
other sounds, Hohanness' terrible cough. Stavros
hears this, and suddenly he has an impulse to stop
and delay the official so that he too will hear the
cough. Then, just as the official gets real close,
Stavros turns and faces the side wall of the corridor. He has controlled his impulse to betray
his friend. He now flattens his face against the
wall. The health official passes by Stavros, entering the doorway behind.

Stavros, face to wall, still shakes from the excitement of what he almost did. Hohanness,
wildly elated, runs out of the cabin and comes towards Stavros, hysterical with delight and relief.

Hohanness: "Stavros! Stavros!"

Then he begins to cough, this time beyond

control. At the moment he gets to Stavros, his cough overwhelms him. He falls into the arms of his friend, in total collapse.

The door into which the health official disappeared was that of the Ship's Hospital, third class. Now attracted by the terrible coughing, the health official comes to the doorway. Behind him appears the Ship's Doctor. There is no longer any doubt as to what Hohanness' fate will be.

Stavros holds Hohanness. He looks at the official.

In the shoeshine boys' cabin, a conference is going on. All are present. Mr. Agnostis is talking to Stavros.

Mr. Agnostis: "I tell you *I* take you. But read! Here! U.S. Government paper. Where is your name here? Where? You want me in jail?"

Silence. They all sit in silence.

Hohanness: "Take my name. I beg you. Take Hohanness Gardashian."

Mr. Agnostis: "There can't be two of you!! There can't be two Hohanness Gardashians. Give up. Go back together. Keep each other company."

That night celebrations break out all over the ship. Disembarkation is at seven the next morning. It is the last night for the shipboard friendships.

At the prow, Stavros and Hohanness huddle together, their arms around each other's shoulders.

Hohanness: "When?"

Stavros: "As soon as everyone's asleep."

Hohanness: "I won't let you . . ."

Stavros turns and smiles at Hohanness, a smile superior and determined, half scorn, half affection, unswayable.

A swirl of First Class passengers rush to the prow of the ship. The women are in long light-colored dresses.

A Girl: "Oh, Third Class is so romantic!"

Man: "They've got the best part of the ship."

Hohanness: "I mean it. If you go, I go too . . . And I can't swim. I'll hold on to you. I'll call out. I won't let you go. I won't!" He pleads with his friend. "Stavros, please, please don't be crazy. Don't be."

He is weeping.

The celebrants have brought musicians with

them, who now strike up. The First Class begins to waltz.

Stavros is full of envy, anger, and revenge. He leaps up and into the middle of the dancers, doing weird, manic leaps and turns.

Man: "Say, look out there. Look out!"

Stavros leaps and kicks out into the air like an insane man. Savage, uncontrollable cries escape his mouth. All the pain that's been stored up in him for months and months!

Hohanness watches Stavros with absolute love. Now Stavros begins to whirl like the dervishes of Konya, around and around, head tilted on one side, his eyes shining with a fanatical light. Hohanness, never taking his eyes off Stavros, rises slowly. Stavros dances wilder and wilder. More and more desperate! Hohanness turns abruptly and looks over the rail. A sudden impulse. He sees the black water of the bay. Each time this boy has said, "Before it eats me!" he has gently touched his chest with the palm of his right hand. Now he makes this gesture for the last time.

Stavros has won the admiration of the celebrants. They cheer.

Unseen, Hohanness goes over the rail and lets himself drop into the black waters of the bay.

The First Class passengers applaud and cheer Stavros. The moment they do this, he stops. He doesn't want anything from them, not even their admiration. He looks them over with fantastic hostility. Then spits out his "Allah!" and struts off.

Terror overcomes Hohanness in the water. He begins to cough. He goes down, comes up, coughing, his strength ebbing fast. He goes down.

The celebrants follow Stavros, begging him to dance some more, the girls beguiling, flirting with this wild boy, not letting him go.

In the black waters of the bay there is no longer any sign of Hohanness.

Stavros pushes off the celebrants, walks up to where he left Hohanness. He looks around for him, calls softly: "Hohanness, Hohanness!" Softly, gently, "Hohanness."

The First Class is disembarking. A band plays a gay exit march. The Third Class watches. Their turn will come later.

The eight shoeshine boys, now with Stavros instead of Hohanness, are looking up at the passengers of the First Class leaving the ship.

Sophia and Aratoon disembark from the gang-plank. Neither looks back. Stavros expected no goodbye. A tap on his shoulder.

It is Bertha, in a hurry. She extends a paper bag and an envelope.

Bertha: "Here! From Mrs. Kebabian."

She turns and goes. Stavros takes out of the paper sack a man's straw hat. He looks at it, smiles, puts it on. Under his breath he says, "Allah!" Then he opens the envelope. It contains a piece of paper money. Nothing else. Mr. Agnostis and the boys gather around.

Mr. Agnostis: "Ooohhh! Fifty dollars! OOOOHHHH!!!!"

In the immigration shed on Ellis Island, three long lines of people lead to three desks. At one of the desks, the eight shoeshine boys, led by Mr. Agnostis, come up for their turn. Stavros is wearing his straw hat. Mr. Agnostis has papers in hand and now presents them to the Immigration official at this desk. The official has seen Agnostis before.

Official: "Oh, look who's here! And eight more little ones! They keep coming, they keep coming! How are all your little slaves?"

Mr. Agnostis' laugh is a nervous one. The boys stare anxiously.

Official: "Scared to death." He turns to the official at the next desk. "Jack! Who was that fellow—a Greek—we're watching for? Criminal assault was it?"

Stavros watches intently. Mr. Agnostis bends over, pretending to tie his shoelace. He has palmed a ten dollar bill and is preparing to slide it towards the shoe of the official, who raises it ever so slightly off the floor. Meantime . . .

Jack: "On the yellow sheet—that's it."

Stavros is watching the ten dollar bill and the foot of the official.

Stavros: "Allah!"

It's not much of a sound. It's rather a kind of growl. But it does voice protest. His dream is being shattered.

The official looks at Stavros. Then he smiles in a peculiarly combative manner. He picks up the yellow sheet.

Official, mispronouncing it of course: "Stavros Topouzoglou. Any of you go by that name?"

Mr. Agnostis: "That fellow died last night."

Official: "You? What's your name?"

He is looking at Stavros again.

Mr. Agnostis: "Hohanness."

Official: "Not you, *you!* He talks doesn't he? What's your name?"

Stavros now has the idea: "Hohanness Gardashian."

Official: "You want to be an American?"

Mr. Agnostis: "Oh yes, sir. Yes, sir."

Official: "Well, the first thing to do is change that name? You want an American name, boy?"

Mr. Agnostis is indicating to Stavros to agree, but Stavros doesn't quite understand.

Stavros, vehemently: "Hohanness Gardashian."

Official: "I know, I know."

Stavros, almost a shout: "Hohanness!"

Official, quickly: "That's enough! Hohanness. That's all you need here."

He writes something on a piece of paper and hands it to Stavros.

Official: "Here! Can you read?"

Stavros, of course, cannot. Mr. Agnostis comes up and reads: "Joe Arness." Then he gets it. "Hohanness. Joe Arness. Hohanness." He turns to Stavros. "Joe Arness. Joe."

Stavros, repeating: "Joe."

Mr. Agnostis: "Arness."

Stavros: "Arness."

Mr. Agnostis, points to him: "Joe Arness."

Stavros, nodding acknowledgment: "Joe Arness."

Mr. Agnostis, to official: "Good!"

Stavros, to official: "Joe Arness."

Official, full of the pride of authorship: "You like it?"

Stavros nods, makes signs, etc.: "Joe Arness, Joe Arness, good, good!"

Official: "Well boy, you're reborn. You're baptized again. And without benefit of clergy. Next!"

Mr. Agnostis and the eight boys leave for the ferryboat to Manhattan. The Ellis Island immigration shed is empty now except for the three officials. They are looking at one object: Stavros' hamal's harness.

Second Official: "What the hell is that?"

Official: "Oh, something one of them left behind."

ῼῼῼ

On the ferry.

Stavros: "So . . . it's the same here!? He took money!"

Mr. Agnostis: "People take money everywhere. But did you see him jump when you spoke? Did you see him jump?"

Stavros: "Yes. Allah!"

Mr. Agnostis laughs. And now Stavros joins in, the first full, simple, free laugh heard from the boy since he left home. Now the others join in, all laughing.

Down the last gangplank come the eight boys and Mr. Agnostis. Stavros first. He falls on his knees and kisses the ground! Then he lifts up and releases a tremendous shout of joy.

7

The first thing we're aware of is an echo, many times magnified, of the shout that Stavros released on American soil. The Topouzoglou family, in Anatolia, is gathered around Isaac. The family has shouted as one. Then the sense of caution that is always with them.

Isaac: "Shshshh! Shshshsh!"

He looks around to see who's within earshot.

Isaac: "Shshsh." Then, almost a whisper, he says: "And here is fifty dollars."

Vasso whispers: "How much is that? Fifty dollars?"

Isaac: "In Turkish money that is . . . that is . . ." He gives up trying to compute. "How did he ever earn so much, so quickly?" Then he answers the question. "America, America!"

Vasso: "Read it again—the last part."

Isaac: " 'In some ways it's not different here—' "

Vasso: "Shsh, not so loud!"

Isaac, looking around: "There's no one."

Vasso: "You never can tell. Go on."

Isaac starts to read again in a cautious tone: " 'It's not different . . .' " He puts the letter down. "How quickly he's forgotten what it is here!" He reads again: " 'But let me tell you one thing. You have a new chance here! For everyone that is able to get here, there is a fresh start. So get ready. You're all coming. I'm working for that. To bring you all here, one by one.' "

Eight boys shine shoes in the Agnostis Shoeshine Parlor in New York, as customers wait. Stavros expertly snaps his polish cloth, a signal for his customers to step down. Stavros is wearing his straw hat. As the customer steps down, Stavros subtly intrudes himself, so that the customer can't avoid tipping.

Customer: "Here you are, Joe."

Stavros grabs the dime, throws it into the air, bounces it off the back of his hand, catches it, squeezes it, pockets it. Then he sings out.

Stavros: "Next! Come on you, let's go you! People waiting!"

In Anatolia, the entire family is leaning over the top of the wall in front of their home. They are all looking up the road, all looking in the same direction.

Suddenly, at full gallop down the road in front of the Topouzoglou home, a squadron of Turkish cavalry raises a heavy dust. For a moment, nothing can be heard except the thunder made by the horses.

The family is all there: Isaac, Vasso, the four sons, the three daughters, even the aunts and the old uncle. They watch as the cavalry rides by and is gone. And then there passes between the members of the family the most subtle and intimate smile. For they share a secret and they share a hope that no one else in this world has. And they all hear in their imaginings, nearer and nearer, louder, Stavros' voice: "Come on you! Let's go you! People waiting! People waiting!"

We see their waiting faces.

And then, at a distance, Aergius, the huge still mountain with its peak of eternal snow.

The End

PC1030
60c

MORTE D'URBAN

WINNER OF THE 1963 NATIONAL BOOK AWARD FOR FICTION

J. F. POWERS

The provocative story that has been called "The best novel written in America since John O'Hara's *Appointment in Samarra*"
—George Frazier, Boston Herald

POPULAR LIBRARY 60c